BODY
IN THE
CANAL

MIKE KENNEDY

Book design copyright © 2023.
Project Manager and Team Coordinator: Mary Cindell Lynn Pilapil
Cover Design by Jim Villaflores
Interior Design by Joseph Apuhin

Published in the United States of America

ISBN: 978-1-7339772-5-8
Crime drama
January 6, 2023

The Mark Springfield Trilogy
Espionage/Thriller (Fiction)

The HUUT is book 1 in the
Mark Springfield trilogy

It revolves around the Huntsville Unit, a unique satellite that has the ability to image deep beneath the surface of the earth. When China reveals its knowledge of the HUUT's existence, the CIA plants an operative. Unknown to the CIA, Russia has her own spy working within their very midst.

It is an intriguing espionage novel that examines the high stakes involved when both China and Russia attempt to steal American satellite technology and the extent to which a country's agent will go in order to return to his homeland as a hero.

Red Fortress ob der Tauber is book
2 in the Mark Springfield trilogy

Ramous Bohdan, one of the CIA's top operatives, has a decision to make. Wait and leave Russia with the information he has been sent to obtain or leave with a secret he has just received from a long-retired KGB agent. The new information is so powerful that it will shatter the already fragile relationship between Russia and the United States.

Unbeknownst to Ramous, a beautiful Russian agent is stalking him.

Learn the special tie the retired KGB agent had with President John F. Kennedy and how it could have changed the course of American history.

Blind Allegiance is book 3 in the Mark Springfield trilogy

Discover how Secret Societies, Benjamin Franklin, and the financial institutions all played their part in weaving the fabric of global corruption. And why the assassination of President Abraham Lincoln allowed it to continue.

And learn what had made the CIA's top operative, Mark Springfield, use his pistol to shoot down the very airplane in which he was traveling.

The Mark Springfield trilogy is action-packed, suspenseful, and thrilling with deep-rooted characters that pull you into the world of the CIA. Once you start reading, you will not want to put the books down.

Satellites, motorcycles, firearms, submarines, and deadly, beautiful women are seamlessly woven into modern times using historical events. Mike's ability to weave real-life events with fictional characters will leave you wondering if his stories are more non-fiction than fiction.

The Space Between Time Sci-fi -Young Adult

Seventeen-year-old Pete Hess's summer project, digging up what he thought was the town's long-lost time capsule, turned into the biggest discovery of his young life.

Suddenly, a million years stands between him and a person he believes to be his older self.

Now Pete must return to a period he understands, and bring together his two selves, but first he must navigate the space between time.

BODY IN THE CANAL

The five Honolulu police cars, three east of McCully Street and two West, parked on Ala Wai boulevard, told me that the police pointing, and peering into the canal could only be looking at one thing, a body.

Yeah, I had a bad feeling. I slowly steered my rental around the parked cruisers, made a slow right turn, and drove over the canal, two blocks up, I made a quick U-turn and headed back towards the bridge. One of the police officers held a roll of yellow tape in his hand and I knew it would not be long before the police rerouted traffic, so I stopped, and like any nosey, ballsy citizen asked, "Hey, whatcha find?"

He pulled up is thick black gun belt, shifted it back and forth before he spoke.

"Sir, please move along."

"Sir, please move along!" Seriously, how many cop shows have you watched? I wondered while letting out an audible grunt.

Quickly, I pulled her blue 'I love Waikiki' hat down low, shifted the car into park and stepped from the pushed open door. I pointed over the concrete wall and stepped closer, straining to see what had brought no less than ten cops to the water at seven in the morning.

"Sir, you really need to get back in your car."

But, I couldn't... There she was, half submerged, slowly rising up and down on the small swells, the water pushing her lifeless body against the rocky bank. Her long, black hair spread out across her back. It was her death bloom.

I had searched for hours, well since 2am when she slapped my face. I let her...I deserved it. Her slap left a small scratch on my left cheek. Unconsciously, in the seconds that I watched her in the water, I rubbed it. It would take time for them to find out who she was, if they scraped under her fingernails, they would find out who I am.

"Get back in your car!"

I didn't notice, but the officer had walked over. He put his hand on my shoulder and gave a not-too-friendly command. "Either get in your car or I'll put you in 'my' car."

I jerked away from his hand. Oh, by the way, I do not like being touched.

I slowly looked over at the young officer. It was all I could do not to launch one of my smart-ass comments, or ball up my fist and slug him. I turned my scratched cheek away from his view, kept my head low, mumbled an apology and walked back to my car. I noticed that they had already wrapped their yellow crime scene tape across the bridge, and by the time I was shifting my car into drive, I was the only one on the bridge without a rack of flashing lights.

While slowly pulling away from the concrete wall, I watched as a small black van park adjacent to the bridge. CORONER had been stenciled in big, bold white letters across the side. I drove slowly, watching a thin, black man, dressed in a blue jumpsuit, step from the van carrying a large camera. I left just in time.

I'll tell you a secret... I really can't remember what I did after she left me. Her slap hadn't taken me by surprise, like I said... I deserved it. This wasn't the first time I had been slapped. Before you ask what I had done to merit a good smack, let me just say it was what I had said. No woman wants to be called a bitch, even if she is. Allow me to explain.

My name is Richard Maxim. I'm a private eye. It's an old term, but I'm an old guy and although my name may match my persona, I have never hit a woman, even if they deserved it. Oh, I've smacked around a few guys, but I won't touch the weaker sex. However, I will speak my peace, and so when Mrs. Tully asked why her husband was cheating on her, I told her, and she didn't like it.

Perhaps I was a little crass, but when someone hires you to get the goods on their supposed loved one and then follows you to Oahu only to yammer on about how poorly you're doing your job, the one you have been doing for forty-five years... Well, I felt bad for the poor sap married to her. And seeing her in the water, I felt bad for her too, but at least she was now quiet.

1

et's turn the clock back three days to Wednesday when I received an email inquiring about my services. I don't like receiving questioning emails from people I don't know. I know, it is a generation thing. I want to meet people face to face. I politely asked her to come into the office, and she agreed, telling me she lived in North Hollywood. I live in Moorpark, California, a good forty miles from Hollywood. It's far enough away from the belly of the beast, but not out of reach for some of the rich and famous. Years ago, I did a little thing for Steve McQueen. He was a great guy, and I'd like to think we would have become friends, but as you probably know he died in nineteen eighty. I have also walked the red-light district in Amsterdam looking for a missing person whom, as it turned out, did not want to be found. And I can tell you, a guy wearing a trench coat fits right in. However, that is a story for another time, back to my client.

Tully emailed me pictures, which I had printed. I need to hold something in my hand. It's why I like books and not electronic readers, but I digress.

The pictures were of her husband, and woman she thought he was seeing. Underneath each photo was a name, Luciano Tully, in parentheses was the name Lou. An eight-and-a-half-by-eleven sheet followed it. It was a real laundry list of the where and when. I had seen this before. I was being used as the third party, someone not related to document the affair. I smelled money, and plenty of it. The problem was, the pictures were from another private dick. I could tell from the shots the person who had taken these photos knew what they were doing. They were good, very telling, the camera steady, the angles through the windows were perfect.

This was not a jealous wife out taking pictures of her cheating husband, it had been someone unassociated with the affair. I could tell all of that from a few pictures. I'm good at what I do, and I don't mind saying it.

Elizabeth Tully stepped into my office and swept her long, coal black hair back over her shoulders with both hands. Two thin straps dangled a small black purse over her left arm. Her soft voice floated across the room from ruby red lips set on a perfectly shaped oval face.

"Mr. Maxim?"

I stood - I hear it's the polite thing to do - and said, "Mrs. Tully, I presume?"

The long-legged beauty strutted across my wooden floors with both hands resting on her hips. After abruptly stopping in front of my desk she said, "I'll need your services so a judge will see what my lying, cheating husband has been up to."

No Hi, no How do you do, no Isn't the weather grand today? I mused. I motioned towards a green tweed, floral printed recliner, not overly stuffed, just a handsome pair of chairs sitting side by side. They had been my grandmother's, and I proudly used them in my office. I guess they helped me feel close to the one person I truly cared for.

"Please have a seat," I said.

Only she didn't. She just stared at me with two perfectly shaped blue eyes. She crossed her arms over her white dress and paced from one side of my office to the other, finally saying,

"You will have to get everything you can." She turned, glared at me, and continued, "And do it quickly. I have a hearing in two weeks."

I had a few questions, but instead, I quietly gathered the pictures, stuffed them all in a manila envelope and slid them across my desk. "Take these," I said. "Consider them a gift from an uninterested PI." I'm not an ambulance chaser; I have more than enough work. However, what happened next gave me pause. Her arms fell to her sides and she abruptly sat down in one of my chairs. Her shoulders slumped so hard I could almost hear them fall. She tried to speak, but her throat choked with emotion.

Finally, she said, "Why? Why does this keep happening?"

I wanted to tell her, but now was not the time. I sat back and waited; I hear I'm a good listener as well.

"You are not the first investigator I have talked to."

She rubbed her hands on her face and continued by pointing at the envelope. "Those were taken by a Ms. Jessica Sleeman. She was number four."

"And I am?" I inquired.

She looked away from the envelope and stared at the top of my desk and hesitantly said, "Number five."

Well so much for any delusions of grandeur.

I shook off being number five. It was easy. I'm not listed on the first page in the phone book. However, Jessica is listed after me, which caused me to question the woman's rational so I asked, "Who put you onto Ms. Sleeman?" It really didn't matter. I was just curious.

"After the first three, who were men, I looked for a woman thinking she would be more... understanding, and treat me better."

"How did that work out for you?" I asked, but I already knew.

She quickly answered, "She isn't a very nice person, and not very understanding."

Inwardly I laughed and almost laughed aloud. If there is one thing you should know, know this:

Ms. Sleeman, Jessica, is the female version of me. I met Jessica almost seven years ago during an investigation for the D.A. Yeah, he hires me from time to time. I was sticking my nose into some, let's say, seedy places and needed someone to use as a diversion. I used a woman. I'm not a chauvinist, but I've known for a long time that women can go almost anywhere.

They cause men to pause, not pay attention, and yes, allow them into places they would never let a man they didn't know. Add a short dress and the right perfume and men turn to putty. I have seen it in Vietnam, pretty girls would come into the clubs, rub up against some of the boys, and the poor saps would give them anything they wanted, even the location of their last hand grenade.

They were spies. That was my job to make sure these women got the "right information," disinformation as we called it. Officially, I was an army major, and it allowed me unfettered access, but I was anything from an army private to an Air Force Colonel. My desk drawer was full of military insignias, patches, gold bars, oak leaves, and stars, whatever it took to turn me into whomever I needed to be. However, slipped into the nineteen-forties-style shoulder holster that was hanging from the coat hook behind my desk was the same gun I wear to this day.

I had smuggled my Colt 1911, semi-automatic pistol out of that godawful country in nineteen seventy-three. I was twenty-six. I had seen things that no man should ever see. And did I sleep with women? Well, first, let's not call it sleep. I had sex with women with the intent of spreading false information, information that they thought they were getting out of me in return for sex. It was a game I had to make them think they were winning, the unwitting American far from home and lonely. They played the game well, made you think you needed to impress them to sleep with them. Impressing them meant showing your importance by how much you knew. Knowing how one's adversaries think and operate is the first step towards defeating them. OK, enough about Vietnam, because aside from getting shot in the neck and the dreams that faded after fifteen years, I had made it back while others, some of them friends, hadn't been so lucky.

2

I studied Elizabeth Tully's defeated look for several long minutes wondering if this was all an act. Was her pouting, pushed out, perfectly shaped lips meant to make me feel sorry for the wounded dove with the broken wing? I sat back in my black leather, swivel chair and rubbed my fingers together in small circles trying not to let my eyes drift south. "I get seventy an hour plus expenses," I blurted, then added, "I'll need five thousand up-front."

"Thank you, Mr. Maxim," she said while standing and reaching out her hand.

A handshake, a binding agreement. I thought, I hesitated, but took it.

After the first shake she said coldly, "I knew you would see it my way."

Her comment irked me because I did not listen to my inner voice. I was right, she was playing the wounded dove. I slapped a pen on top of a notepad, slid it across my desk and said, "I need to know what your husband does for a living. Jot down all of your information, banks, credit cards, and credit bureau, all of it. And that means usernames, passwords, whatever I need to gain access. I'll need to take a picture of your driver's license as well." I swiveled my chair around to the whiteboard that stood on an easel behind me. I picked up the black marker and, while writing, I said, "Your time started when you walked in." I wrote 4 PM, August 8th, 2013, in the upper left corner of the board. I know, I was being a dick, but so was she. When I turned around, I saw sitting on my desk her license, which I quickly photographed.

"I'm sure you will take cash," she said in a condescending tone.

"Cash is king," I quickly replied. I watched her count out hundreds from a stack of bills and neatly lay them on the manila folder. The money flowed easily from her hand and the more I watched her, the more I disliked her, so I gave myself a raise. "After 5 PM, I get overtime, so that'll be a C-note."

She gave me a stern look and finished counting out the bills.

"Here's ten thousand. I'll assume that will buy me your undivided attention."

Here's what I learned from my stint in Vietnam: the more sex you have, the less it means to you. The same holds true for money. The more you have, the less it means. It was clear Elizabeth Tully had a lot of money.

She pushed the note pad back across the desk and said, "I'll email you my banking and credit card information." She turned, turned back, paused, and then added, "I'll assume you will be very discreet with my accounts."

"I assure you, I have no interest in your balances outside of how it pertains to my investigation. I want to know who is spending what and where it is being spent," I shot back. I glanced down at the notepad and asked, "Your husband is a bank president?"

"That's what I wrote. I will be contacting my lawyers and banks just to be on the safe side."

Aren't we off to a grand start! I thought. "Good day, Mrs. Tully." I stood and watched her walk through the doorway. She was a beautiful woman, but unfortunately it was only skin deep. Perhaps I am the only one who sees this, or do, so called, friends avoid her like the plague?

3

I picked up my cell phone and turned it over in my hand while wondering if money had changed my new client. I took a few short steps to the window and watched her walk out of my building. She slipped into the backseat of a white Mercedes which quickly pulled away from the curb. The windows were tinted, but I knew she was watching me.

I scrolled through my address list, stopped at Jessica's number, and pressed the phone icon. After three rings, I got a not-too-friendly voice.

"Richard."

I'm sure she wanted to call me something else.

"What do I owe the pleasure of your call?"

Hmmm... She was pleasant, but 'pleasure' of my call? Did she forget I had stood her up?

"Let me guess, this is the phone call I never got, telling me that you never intended to actually meet me for dinner?"

There it is. "I'm sorry. I simply forgot," was all I could say.

"What can I do for you, Dick?"

"What do you know about Elizabeth Tully?"

"I fired her!"

"That's crass. But... I hear she fired you." Yeah, I was prodding her.

"She's full of shit. I was on the case long enough to snap a few photos and get a bad feeling...a very bad feeling."

I've known Jessica for a long time, and she is not one to quit anything. But I heard something else, a quiver in her voice, which piqued my interest. I moved forward in my seat, pushed the phone to my ear, and asked, "Jessica... Did something happen?" I waited for an answer. In fact, I waited for a while, and then suddenly...the line went dead.

I tossed the phone on my desk while leaning back in my chair. I half-looked at the pictures that hung around my office while thinking about the call. I stared at my prized possession, an autographed movie poster given to me by The King of Cool, Steve McQueen. I asked his character, Lt. Frank Bullitt, what would make Jessica act that way, but my question went unanswered. He quietly stared back while standing behind a line of cars, the last one being the famous nineteen-sixty-eight dark green Mustang fastback. His Colt Diamondback snub-nosed revolver hung from an old-style leather shoulder holster.

Suddenly, rolling thunder rattled my windows and bright flashes of light lit up my office, causing me to turn away from the poster. With my foot, I kicked off the desk, rolling my chair over to the open window. Rain blew through the screen, but I had it closed before the downpour.

No rain until tomorrow, I thought. Why can't the weather guys ever get it right?

I set my gaze back onto McQueen and said, "I need to take a drive."

I don't mind driving. In fact, I kind of like it. It settles my mind. I pushed up from my chair, then grabbed my suit coat from an old five-armed, freestanding wooden rack and pulled it on. Hung next to it was my beige double-breasted trench coat. I slipped my arms into the sleeves, pulled it over my suit coat, and then turned up the collar. Although not cold, it was a bit of a walk to my car.

Before I left my office, I looked through the blinds and peered out into the street. Unfortunately, the glare from the streetlights made it difficult to see through the rain-streaked windows. As I walked through the doorway, I snatched my hat from a hook to the right of the doorframe. It's a tan fedora, trimmed with a black band. I set it on my head with a slight forward tilt to the right.

Today, my attire is a dark blue pinstripe suit, white shirt, black tie, and a shoulder-holstered firearm to top it off. Yeah, I'm a private eye, might as well look the part.

4

Jessica lived twenty minutes south of me and you can guess why I wanted to see her. I needed to find out what spooked a tough private eye.

When I arrived, I passed slowly by her office only to continue onto her house after I noticed the closed shades and no back light. I parked a block away. I don't know why; I just had a feeling.

The rain had lightened up a bit, but with the low clouds, it was dark, so I grabbed a small flashlight that I kept in the door's side compartment and slipped it into my pocket. I pushed open the door, slid off the seat, and quickly stepped up onto the sidewalk. I stared in the direction of her house while adjusting my hat. After glancing up and down the street, I walked toward her residence, but stopped cold when I heard the gunshot.

It was a single shot and it made me quicken my pace until I covered most of the distance. Then I slowed and studied the houses around me. I watched curtains being pulled to the side. A door opened to my right and I froze.

A hushed female voice asked, "Was that a gunshot?"

"It sure sounded like it," I answered. I looked up at her and added, "You might want to go back inside."

Around the corner and two houses up was Jessica's residence. As I rounded the bend, I saw someone leaving the house and walking quickly toward a car. It didn't take long, but I recognized the tall, thin subject.

I took a few rushed steps closer and yelled, "Jess!"

She turned, after a few long seconds said, "Jesus, Richard!" Pointing to the car, she said, "Quick! Get in!"

By the time I had closed the door, the engine was running, and she was shifting into drive.

"I was just coming to see you," she offered.

In her hand, she held a square, white envelope, the kind you would send a thank-you card in.

"I have to explain, but not over the phone."

"Wait a minute, did I hear a gunshot?"

After straightening the car, she looked at me and in a quivering voice said, "I never had to kill someone." After a long pause, she added, "Tonight... I did."

* * *

I could tell she was rattled. However, before I had a chance to say anything she shook the envelope in front of me and in a shaky voice said, "take this."

I took the envelope from her trembling hand and pulled up the flap that had been tucked inside the opening. I partially pulled out three pictures and a folded piece of paper and quickly looked at them, then at her.

"That's my dad." Jessica said. "He's in an assisted living home up in Ventura."

She looked back at me, her lip starting to quake.

"Take a breath," I said while rubbing my hand across her shoulder. I waited for her to compose herself.

Finally, she said, "I didn't take those pictures, no one I knew took those pictures. I don't know where those came from."

In the lights of the oncoming traffic, I could see tears running down her cheeks. I knew what was coming, and all I could do was wait. She needed to process killing someone. It's not like the movies.

"Hey, I have an idea, let's pull over," I offered with a smile while pointing to a distant grocery store's parking lot. "Jessica let me drive for a while."

"No, no, I'm fine," she said in a faint voice.

"Jessica, no...you are not. Your driving is erratic, and it may not be the best idea to get pulled over by the police."

Quickly, she looked at me. Jess was wearing a blue hooded windbreaker, but with her sleeves hiked up to her elbows, and her hands on the steering wheel, I could see blood on her right hand and down her arm. I motioned by a tilt of my head.

Her eyes locked onto the blood and she could not look away.

When we crossed over the centerline, into oncoming traffic I thought, *oh shit!* thank God for the oncoming car, and its wailing horn that startled her. She jerked the wheel and overcorrected, the car lurched back into the lane and then out, I thought for sure I was going to die. Finally, Jessica regained control.

Moments later, she pulled into the parking lot and into a designated spot on the other side of the property. After shifting the car into park, she dropped her head onto the steering wheel and sobbed.

I looked around to make sure we had not caught anyone's attention and after a few minutes, I offered, "you tell me where we are going and I'll take us there." After several long seconds, she finally offered, "He was so close when I pulled the trigger."

After a minute, she turned her head, rested it on the steering wheel, and stared at me. After taking a few long, shaky breaths she uttered, "he was going to kill me."

"Jessica, you are okay now. You are with me."

Slowly she pushed off the steering wheel and sat upright. After wiping her face with both hands, she continued, "I was on my way to see you. I wanted to explain. Those pictures are of my dad," she said with a slight nod toward the envelope.

I took the three pictures out of the envelope and looked at them one by one. In each picture, an older man was sitting, reading a book. In each photograph, he held a different title in his hand, the first having a dark-colored cover with a picture of a satellite. Across the top the words, THE HUUT, were boldly printed. The photograph had been taken outdoors while the person was sitting in a lounge chair, an intense look frozen on his face. In two of the pictures, he was sitting on a small couch in a room, each time with a different book in his hand. On one, the book cover was brown with a hand from an unseen body gripping a bloody old-style watch. The words RED FORTRESS OB DER TAUBER was scribed across the bottom. The third and final book had a brightly colored cover. It was of a jet ripped open by an explosion, and BLIND ALLEGIANCE was prominently displayed across the top. "I see your dad is a reader, but wh -"

"I gave my dad those books as a gift. That trilogy was supposed to keep him occupied for a while. But, that's the thing, he read those in two days. I..."

"No, I get it. Someone was obviously close to your dad, too close." I thought for a moment, then said, "Your dad may be in danger, but it's odd that the staff let whomever in to photograph him, and then later allowed that person to return?"

"Read the note."

I unfolded the piece of paper, quickly read the one line, looked at Jessica, and said, "Now I know where we're going... Ventura." Written on the slip were the words, 'Stop now and he lives.'

I pushed open my door, stepped out of the car, and changed spots with Jessica. After leaving the parking lot, I said, "Lay the seat back, close your eyes, and find your happy place." She just looked at me and bunched her eyebrows. However, she rolled her head back towards the passenger door and closed her eyes. It was no use. The person she killed would haunt her dreams for years to come.

5

After checking in on her dad, who was asleep, we inquired with the staff about any visitors that he had had. No one knew of any guests outside of the normal residents of the facility.

*   *   *

The Plaza Hotel sits just yards from the beach, and I knew it would be a good place for my friend to lay low. We both needed a few days, her to rest and me to find out what was going on, and figure out just who the hell Luciano Tully was.

We had a few drinks in the lounge, and like the gentleman I am, I escorted her to the room. And before you get any big ideas, Jessica and I are just friends, co-workers, if you will. My drive back to my office in Moorpark was roughly thirty minutes. I did not want to waste any time, so I placed a call to a detective I knew. He answered on the second ring, in his deep baritone, authoritative voice.

"Homicide, Detective Vanderwerff."

"Shawn, it's Dick Maxim."

"Don't you ever sleep," he asked.

"I could say the same thing about you." Quickly I glanced at my watch and thought, t*en o'clock*.

"What can I do for you, buddy?" he queried.

"I have an off-the-record question."

Laughter filled my phone's speaker. "What would surprise me is if you didn't ask an 'off-the-record' question," Shawn quipped.

"Nature of the beast, my friend."

Let me tell you about Shawn. He likes to drink. Not too much, but a bottle of good Scotch goes a long way. I learned that after our first meeting. We've been friends for a while; however, our first encounter almost landed me in jail. I pushed by him at a crime scene, his crime scene. He was standing on the spectator side of the yellow tape. I nudged by him - Okay, perhaps it was a little more than a nudge - lifted up the tape, and stepped into an area I really didn't belong, but laying fifteen feet in front of me, shot three times, was a woman I had earlier had a heated argument with. What I didn't know was, Shawn was playing the onlookers. It's a thing he does, arrives after the tape goes up and works the gathered crowd. Bad guys like to return to the scene of the crime, so he looks for that one person lingering in the crowd too interested, or sweating bullets. A uniformed officer turned me around towards the tape sending me right back to the person I had just pushed past. He gave me a hard stare, and suddenly, I felt cold inside. He reached inside his tailored dark blue suit jacket, pulled out his gold badge, and let it hang from a Yuengling lanyard. It wasn't only his six-foot solid frame that was intimidating, he had a presence. Shawn Vanderwerff was a clean-cut, professional law-man who means business.

"You are?" he evenly asked.

"Richard Maxim. I'm a private investigator." I decided not to be a smart ass. There's a time and place, this was neither. I motioned towards my pocket and asked, "May I?" He nodded, I reached in, pulled out a small silver case, and offered a business card, to which he gave a quick glance.

"Mind telling me why my victim is holding one of your business cards?" With a backward nod, he continued, "Do you know why I was standing over there?"

I knew the question was rhetorical, so I waited for the answer.

"I want to know if anyone is too interested in my crime scene. The depraved do that, they stay out on the periphery, reliving their activities. I never had one actually walk back into the crime scene."

You can guess, it went downhill from there. However, that's another story and it was more than a dozen years ago.

"Shawn, have you been busy tonight?" I inquired.

"No, just going over some older cases looking for missed clues."

"Slow night then?" I pressed.

"Very!" After a slight pause he said,

"I'm not even going to ask, but Dick… let me know if you need me. And besides, I enjoy hearing about your cases. I live vicariously through you. PIs can get away with stunts that would get us kicked off the force."

"Thanks, Shawn," I said with a chuckle.

No one had called the police about the gunshot in Jessica's neighborhood. It didn't surprise me, folks live in fear. Jessica's encounter had gone unreported. Now, back to my office, and my computer for a little follow-up.

Waiting for me in my inbox was the information from Mrs. Tully. Along with it were documents from two of her lawyers threatening legal action for any abuse of her accounts. *Give me a break!* I opened up six credit card statements, and one bank account statement that struck me as odd. It was a joint account with only five thousand dollars in it. I perused the accounts and stopped at a Delta airline ticket charge on one of the credit cards. Written next to the airline name was the thirteen-digit ticket number. Next stop, the Delta site. By clicking the 'My Trips' icon, I easily found the flight associated with the number. It turned out there were two tickets purchased one week ago. Departing Los Angeles, California this Friday morning at eight-fifteen, arriving in Honolulu, Hawaii, just before noon. Sometimes this is just too easy.

I picked up my phone and dialed my newest client, inwardly happy to make the call especially since it was approaching midnight. Her phone rang long enough that I expected to leave a message, but there she was, answering in a sleepy, seductive voice. I pictured her wearing a pair of loose shorts, a top pulled to one side exposing a bare, smooth shoulder. Her long black hair a mess. I imagined her pushing up one side as she spoke into the phone. I know, guys are pigs.

"Hello."

"Mrs. Tully, it's Dick Maxim."

After a long pause, she said, "This better be God damn important!"

Hmmm... testy, I thought with a devilish grin. "What do you know about an upcoming trip your husband has planned?"

"To where?" she snapped.

"I'd rather not say?" I didn't need her interfering.

"Nothing. I know nothing of any trip. Is he taking his whore?"

Well, so much for sleepy and seductive... she was fully awake now. "Mrs. Tully, I'll look into this and let you know what I find." I was polite, but quickly hung up. Now for the real question: who is Luciano Tully? He's a banker and has money; at least his wife doles it out as if he does, so he must have some social status. My guess was he would be easy to find.

I typed his name in the search bar and seconds after hitting the enter key, there he was, tanned skin, a head of thick black hair, maybe five-eight, in his mid to late forties and not dressed as I thought a bank president would dress. A dark green polo, neatly tucked into tan Dockers. He was surrounded by five women, none of them his wife. However, one of them, a Caucasian platinum blonde, appeared to have her arm tightly slipped through his. The other four were gorgeous, but the blonde, there was something about her. She wore a tight, strapless, ankle-length silver dress, finished with a pair of black heels. Her hair, perfectly parted down the middle and straight as an arrow, cascaded down to her waist. It contrasted the other women's shoulder-length, jet-black styles. *Is this what money gets you*, I thought.

Hmmm... Finding out what was going on in Hawaii was proving to be a little more challenging. However, nature called, so the search had to wait.

I walked into the small bathroom, did what I needed to do, and returned to find someone casually sitting in one of my grandmother's chairs. Since my doors were locked, I was taken off guard, but I didn't show it. I calmly sat down, but sternly asked, "Who are you? More importantly, how did you get in here?" He was a large man, not a fat man, but solid. He wore a dark fitted suit, and if I had to guess, I would guess him a bit younger than me, a head of gray hair tends to show one's age.

"Mr. Maxim, it's not important who I am." He nodded at my left side and said, "You will not need that 1911. I would leave it holstered."

Although the stranger had a *presence,* and his voice had a touch of authority, I did not feel threatened. "What brings you to my office at this time of night, uninvited I might add?" He probably held a gun in his unseen right hand, but gun or not, I do not like these kinds of surprises.

"You have been asked to look into Luciano Tully," he responded evenly.

"That's client, PI privileged information," I offered.

He narrowed his gray eyes, and with a dismissive wave of his hand, he said, "Be it as it may, stop. He is already being investigated."

"I should probably mention that I don't like being told what to do, especially from strangers who break into my office," I shot back. You can guess I wasn't very happy.

"Mr. Maxim, this is bigger than you can imagine. Having someone else poking around may muddy the waters. I'd hate to see you get hurt, or wind up dead."

"Is that a threat?"

"Not at all. I'm not a killer."

"But I sense you have killed." I can smell death, and he reeked of it.

"Perhaps," he answered with a slight nod. He regarded me for a brief moment and then stood, turned, and walked towards the door. Over his shoulder, he added, "You were born on flag day in forty-seven. You went in country in nineteen sixty-nine, you left in seventy-three, worked intel. I hear you were good at it. Private investigator ever since. Like I said, Mr. Maxim, this is bigger than you can imagine."

He unlocked the door, opened it, and quietly left. Okay, full disclosure, I said I didn't feel threatened, but I was happy he was gone. There was only one thing left to do before I called it a night: purchase my ticket to Hawaii.

6

Later that night, in the comfort of my home, I heard the sounds of breaking glass.

My house is locked up tighter than Fort Knox, so when I heard the glass break, I instantly thought of my earlier visitor. I'll be the first to tell you, no matter how many times I have been through this kind of thing, my heart always races. It's the unknown, the who, the how many in the wee hours.

I rolled off the bed on the side where I keep my shotgun. I keep my Mossberg 590 A1 loaded with twelve-gauge double aught buckshot. And no, I don't rack a shell into the chamber to try'n scare bad guys. I shoot bad guys. So, you know, if you ever decide to sneak up on me, my guns are always loaded, and with one in the pipe.

I looked at my alarm clock, a glowing red 2:30a.m. stared back. I felt my breathing pick up and deliberately slowed it down. I slightly bowed my head, closed my eyes, and focused on the smallest sound. Tires slowly rolling on loose stone behind my house, suddenly a short screech from downstairs. *What was that?* I thought. *It had to be my couch, someone bumped into it. And who the hell is in the car?* I waited, still listening. I wanted them, whoever *them* is, to think I was still sleeping.

I gave them what I thought was enough time to sneak up my stairs, then I shouldered my shotgun, pushed off the safe, slowly laid my finger on the trigger, and waited.

*　*　*

A booming crash, followed by chunks of door flying across my room, told me it was time to send my uninvited guest to hell. As soon as he cleared the splintered frame, I pressed the trigger. A thunderous boom set the stock hard into my shoulder. Pumping the fore-end, I ejected the spent shell, chambered another, pressed the trigger, and made sure I would have to repaint both sides of the room.

I kept the gun shouldered and rushed through my battered doorframe while glancing at the bleeding heap in the corner of my room.

Stepping onto the top landing was a dark figure raising what looked like a semiautomatic handgun; however, mine was up first, and double aught buck in the chest will ruin anyone's day. The blast lifted him up off his feet, and the next time he touched down was on the bottom landing.

I lowered my shotgun, ejected the smoking shell, chambered another, and quickly descended the steps while scanning my downstairs. Once satisfied I was no longer under attack, I poked the masked intruder with the barrel; however, I knew he was dead.

I quickly walked to the back of the house and slowly crept up to the side of the window frame. I moved the curtains enough to see the road. Seeing nothing out of the ordinary, I did the same for the front and then headed upstairs.

I unmasked my intruder, and imagine my surprise to find it was a woman. Not many killers are. But anyone who breaks through my door and points a gun at me is going to get shot. I believe in equal opportunity.

There was something else. She had an earpiece, but not just any earpiece. I recognized it for what it was, a high-tech wireless communication device.

I took it off her ear and slipped it under my mattress. Why? Because of the sirens, and it sounded like I only had a few minutes. I patted her down trying to keep my hands out of her blood. I waited too long, there was a lot of it. I snapped a picture of her with my phone and then quickly walked downstairs and repeated what I had done to the woman, only I stashed his earpiece behind a potted plant. Less than a minute later, my room filled with flashing red and blue lights.

After taking one more look around, I unloaded my shotgun, leaned it up against an adjacent wall, and waited for the knock on my door.

*   *   *

Three and a one-half hours later, I closed and locked my door. I had a mess to clean up, but for the time being, I sprayed some bleach on it. I pulled my nineteen eleven from my small lock box, reloaded the Mossberg, and made myself comfortable in my guest room. I read the time displayed under the TV, six ten. Since I had met Mrs. Tully, Jessica had shot an intruder, her dad had an unknown visitor, I had my own visitor, and then there were my two assassins. I did some quick math. All of the aforementioned in only fourteen and a half hours. This could get interesting.

There's a time when you enter a light sleep, about five to ten minutes after you close your eyes. Your heart rate slows, and your body temperature drops. You're getting ready for a deep sleep. And eventually after a matter of hours, you slip into a deep, restorative sleep. Well, that's not what happened. Apparently, I was destined to only get a couple of hours. Before I could enter REM, something occurred to me. My eyes opened, and I stared up at the ceiling thinking about the picture of Tully and the women. I pushed myself from the bed, retrieved my computer, and typed in

Luciano Tully. Seconds later, I was staring at the same picture of him surrounded by his entourage, and according to the picture on my phone, one of them had been lying on my floor in a bloody heap hours ago. A connection, but why in the hell would she try to kill me?

I looked at the picture of Luciano Tully and the five women who surrounded him with a different eye. Four of them started looking like, like... bodyguards. Well, well, Mr. Tully, did you just try to have me killed?

7

I spent the rest of the day in my house cleaning up the mess, and trying to find out what was going on in Hawaii that would catch the attention of a banker. Other than Hawaii being Hawaii, I found nothing of real interest.

Since Lou Tully knew my identity, I could not risk being seen on the same flight. So, when Friday morning rolled around, I arrived late to the airport, purposely missing my eight-fifteen flight. As expected, I was put on the next airplane to Honolulu.

I played the tourist and strutted through the terminal with my best pink flamingo Hawaiian shirt, jean shorts, and sandals. Slung over my shoulder was a turtle print backpack. And lucky me, sitting four rows from the gate was none other than my employer. I walked past her, turned, sat across from Mrs. Tully, and gave her one of my best *why are you here* looks. She stared back through big, round dark sunglasses. Her coal black hair and ruby red lips accentuated her ankle-length white dress. "Why are you here?" I asked coarsely.

"I need to assure my money is well spent," she blurted.

I tried my best not to raise my voice. "I don't need a babysitter, Mrs. Tully! I have been doing this for a long time."

There was a long pause, and then she uttered, "I need to see her; I need to see the slut my husband is running off with."

This wasn't going to end well. "I don't think it's a good idea for you to be here. Let me collect the information you need for your court appearance. I'll hand everything over to you in a week's time." She shook her head.

Suddenly over the Public Address were the preboarding notices. When the announcement came for first class, we both stood.

"I see I'm paying for your first-class ticket," she said sharply.

"Actually, no. This is my cue to head to the men's room. Is that something you need to supervise, too?" I gave her a hard look, turned, and walked away, thinking, *this is going to ruin Hawaii for me.*

I flew quite a bit and half-expected an upgrade; however, no such luck as first class was full, so back to my aisle seat, thirty-four D, I went. When I walked through the first-class cabin, I paid no attention to Mrs. Tully, but I could feel her eyes following me.

The mood on the plane was light and everyone seemed in good spirits. The flight attendants, with their long flowing Hawaiian dresses and fresh Leis, served Champagne to everyone. I chatted to a couple next to me and learned the reason for the bubbly. It was one of the stewardess' last flights before retiring.

I was complimented several times for my pink flamingo shirt. I don't know why, but I had been seeing the long-necked bird in stores and advertisements everywhere so when I ran across the shirt, I had thought it good luck to purchase it.

When it comes to bourbon, I won't turn it down, breakfast, lunch, a mid-day snack, it's good anytime. Oh, I know what you are thinking, Dick Maxim's a drunk. No, I just like bourbon. Champagne on the other hand is just Champagne. However, when it's free, I won't pass it up. Six or so plastic cups in, I was feeling like the rest of the passengers, a little tipsy.

Our provider of the Champagne, Cassidy, spared no expense; the drinks flowed even after our meal service. We were roughly the same age, so I'd say she had a full career, and by the number of pinches I received on my arm, her libido was nowhere close to retiring. And yeah, she really liked my shirt.

I was picked up once before by one other flight attendant who flirted with me on a trip to Japan. I did not intend to spend the night at the Tokyo International Airport, but after I went through customs and immigration, a very attractive Asian flight attendant was waiting for me. Of course, it was my duty to show good cooperation between our two countries. And I did...several times.

8

During our descent into Honolulu, I wondered how I could ditch my employer who was becoming a pain in the ass. I wanted to put her on a plane back to Los Angeles. As I was plotting, Cassidy handed me a folded napkin while doing the seat belt check. Funny thing is, she didn't care who had seen her. I gave her a coy smile as she walked off. I opened the folded napkin. Written under her name was a phone number along with the days, Friday - Tuesday. I studied her as she walked away. Maybe Hawaii wouldn't be so bad after all.

Fifteen minutes after we touched down, I was walking towards baggage claim in the warm Hawaiian air. There was no sign of Mrs. Tully. Although I thought it strange, I wasn't unhappy. Then suddenly as I walked into the main terminal, I heard, 'Mr. Maxim.'

There she was, sitting in a chair at an empty gate. I thought to continue on, but she looked worried so I decided not to, damn my big heart. I placed my backpack on an adjacent chair and sat across from her.

Not giving me time to ask a question, she immediately leaned in and said, "Since we are going to be working together, I have decided it important to tell you something."

Yeah, I wasn't happy either, but I let her continue. I was seconds away from dumping this job. I'd eat the ticket and whatever expenses I had just to be done with her. *She's the type of person who will get me killed*, I thought.

She stared at me for several awkward seconds, and it seemed she had a change of heart, but then suddenly she blurted, "Eight months ago, my husband took possession of a safe deposit box. At first, he was excited. Then suddenly, as if it had never happened, he stopped talking about it."

She paused, perhaps thinking I had a question, but I said nothing, because I'm such a good listener. Finally, she continued.

"When I curiously mentioned the box, he told me that it had all been a mistake and there was no safe deposit box."

Okay, here's my procedure for questioning people: don't ask questions. When someone wants to talk, and is nervous, and she was very nervous, they will talk. Don't get in their way by asking questions.

"Four months ago, he started getting phone calls at all hours. Phone calls he couldn't take in front of me. When I inquired, as any wife would, he told me they were work-related and very confidential."

She stopped, leaned back in the chair, and stared at me. Finally, she offered, "he's a bank president for god's sake, not the director of national security!"

I had heard enough and coarsely asked, "*So, this get me information for a court date is all bullshit?*"

"I'm sorry! I knew it had something to do with the bank. I never believed it was another woman until I got the pictures from that Jessica Sleeman. Now I don't know what to think."

Unless the pictures were a setup to throw her off track, I thought. "Did you ask your husband if there was another woman?"

"I am not the jealous type, Mr. Maxim!" After a long pause, she quietly added, "But yes, yes, I did."

Now it was my turn to sit back and put my never-trusting mind to work. The first three investigators appeared to blow her off. Jessica took the job, snapped some photos, turned them over to the client, and then mysteriously, her dad was threatened and someone had tried to kill her. And now she was off the case. I bet a paycheck the first three were paid off or threatened in some way. And you know what happened to me. I had a mysterious visitor, then it appeared Mr. Tully tried to have me killed. That would have stopped his wife from looking into this any further. A safe deposit box? How do I get a look at that? "Is the safe deposit box in his bank?" It needed asking.

She looked at me oddly and answered. "I don't know. I just assumed it was."

"If we left tomorrow for Los Angeles, could we get a look inside that box?"

She shook her head, fumbled with her wide brimmed hat, and said, "No, not Saturday." After a slight pause, she added, "Well, not this Saturday. Even the wife of the bank's president needs an appointment."

I sat back, turned, and watched the last of the passengers walk by. I studied their smiling faces, more to make sure no one was *overly* interested in us. "No!" I said with a shake of my head. I turned back toward her and continued, "Let's not ask anyone in advance. It may be better to just show up." All of a sudden, her condescending tone returned, and she blurted,

"Well, I think it's better to make an appointment. That way they will be ready for us."

"Have you ever heard of the Saint Valentine's Day Massacre?" Bear with me; I was trying to make a point.

She stared at me. Finally, she said, "Yes, yes, who hasn't. Some mob men were stood up against a wall and killed in Chicago. I believe in the twenties."

"It happened in nineteen twenty-nine to seven members of Chicago's north side gang. The men were gathered at a Lincoln Park garage, lined up against a wall by four policemen, and gunned down using a pair of Thompson sub-machine guns and two shotguns. It was a mess." I paused for effect, but I was losing her. I leaned in and quickly offered, "But they weren't policemen; they were employed by the legendary Al Capone. The seven men were brought into the garage under false pretenses and killed." She looked at me as if I had horns, so I cut to the chase. "That could happen to us. If you call someone, they will be ready, and like the mob men, we could be walking into a trap and gunned down." I considered telling her of my early morning visitors. I decided not to, though I probably should have. Instead, I let what I had said sink in. After a few long minutes, I stood and said, "Let's go. Your husband is here until next Thursday. We, on the other hand, will be on tomorrow afternoon's flight back to Los Angeles. We are going to get a look inside that box."

She let out a long sigh and stood. We both walked towards baggage claim, but when approaching a rack of hats, Tully stopped and said, "I need one of these."

She snatched the I Love Waikiki baseball style hat from a hook, removed her floppy brimmed cover, and flopped her new hat on her head. After glancing in a mirror, she said, "Pay the man," and walked off.

Elizabeth Tully and I went our separate ways after leaving the airport. I encouraged her to lay low and talk to no one. The safe deposit box added a new twist. I felt its contents were key; it was important to get a look inside. Leaving Oahu Saturday cut down our chances of running into her husband. Plus, I had a hidden agenda.

9

There's something about a tropical breeze. It's a warmth that hugs you from all sides. Perhaps it's the romanticizing of what is to come. In my mind's eye, I could see sailors chasing scantily clad Hawaiian girls down the beach from a time long gone.

From my balcony, I sipped coffee while watching a paddle boarder slowly slice a disappearing path across the water. I returned to my hotel around five Saturday morning. It turned out that Cassidy was older than I am. That hadn't been evident from what went on in her room the previous night. I used that number she handed me and met her for dinner which turned into a night of, well let's just say, memories.

Tully and I arrived at the airport late Saturday morning, and as we walked towards the ticket counter she said, with defiance. "I spoke to Roger!"

I bunched my eyebrows while searching my memory. Finally, I asked, "Who the hell is Roger?"

"My husband's number one man."

I froze, reached out my arm, grabbed her elbow, and squeezed it with my hand until she stopped. "You called someone?!"

"I told you. Roger. I let him know we will arrive tonight. I also made arrangements to see the safe deposit box Monday morning."

"Jesus!" Still squeezing her arm, I turned her around and spat, "I take it you didn't understand my Saint Valentine's Day story?" She tried violently to jerk her arm away, but my grip held fast. I clenched my jaw and waited for her to protest, but she just glared. I led her away from the ticket counter, and through tight lips, I laid it out, saying, "We can't leave now, and until we do, you and I are going to be connected at the hip." I pulled her outside and, with my free hand, hailed a cab. I was sure she didn't like being jerked around. While we waited, I added, "There's something going on here we just don't understand. Jessica, the one you speak poorly of, had a visitor. I'm quite sure it had to do with this case."

"What did he want?" Tully asked rebelliously.

"We'll never know," I said, shaking my head. "She killed him."

*　*　*

Saturday went by quickly. I checked us into my original hotel. Fortunately, they had a suite. Mrs.

Tully ran hot and cold, but I was able to keep her close all day. A little before midnight, I looked in on her to find she was fast asleep. I had spent the day being told my work ethic left quite a bit to be desired, so I hightailed it out of there and went for a walk. I went to the outdoor bar, grabbed a beer, a bourbon and walked towards an outcropping of rocks along the water's edge.

Finally, after four additional trips to the bar, I leaned back on the rocks, fighting droopy eyelids. Suddenly an annoying voice interrupted my listlessness.

"What if he *does* have a girlfriend?"

I forced open my eyes and slowly turned towards the voice, which just so happened to be coming from none other than my client. I failed to stifle my groan, and by the way she pursed her lips at me, I knew she had heard it. "What are you doing out here?"

She took a few steps towards me and asked, "Why do you think my husband is cheating on me?"

I didn't want to say it, but the five bourbons took over. "Because you're a bitch." And that's when I got my slap. Like I said, I deserved it. No one likes to be called a bitch, and I said it like everyone knew it. I watched her walk away and figured she was going back to the room. I lay back and let the beer and bourbon have their way.

The rising tide only allowed me to doze for an hour. I pushed off the rocks and headed back to the room. When I arrived, I looked in on Tully. Her bed was empty. Through the open door I could clearly see into the vacant bathroom. "Elizabeth!" After not getting a response, I walked in just to be thorough. The suite was empty. Elizabeth was gone. "Damn it!"

I grabbed her purse, made my way to the parking garage, and slowly drove my rental through the streets around the hotel, thinking she too needed to get out for a while. I expanded my search, block by block until I spied the hordes of cops, and that brings us back to the canal. I needed to get off this island, and fast. So, with Elizabeth Tully floating in the canal, I called the only person who could help.

10

F ive rings later I began to worry, and just when I thought I was going to need to leave a message, I got a "Hello."

"Jessica." I said quickly. Yes, I'm calling Jessica, I need help, and like I said, she's a tough PI and understands the danger.

After a long pause she asked, "Where are you?"

"Never mind that. How are you?"

"Dick, when I returned home no one was there. I expected to see the police, but it was quiet."

"Did you go back into your house?" I cautiously asked.

"I did, and it was like it had never happened. Not a thing out of place, no body, no blood, nothing. I left and drove around for a bit to make sure I wasn't being tailed, then checked into a hotel five miles away."

When I said this could get interesting, I was right. I let it all sink in, then asked, "Do you own a long, black wig?"

"I have a black wig. It's only shoulder length."

"Get one, meet me at my office tomorrow, noon."

Jessica was taller than my client and this probably wouldn't work, but I needed to find out what the hell was in the safe deposit box that got Mrs. Tully killed, not to mention the attacks on me and Jessica. I hung up and headed straight for the airport.

* * *

My only airline option put me in Los Angeles at eight o'clock at night. The flight was uneventful, and although highly unusual I slept. While deplaning, I grouped with a young family and offered to carry their small stroller from the jet way. I hoisted it onto my shoulder and covered my face. Perhaps an unnecessary precaution, perhaps not.

I left my bags at the hotel in Hawaii so there was no need to go to the lower level. As we approached the down escalator, I set the stroller on the floor next to the restroom and exclaimed I would say hi again at baggage claim. The father popped it open, thanked me, and went on his way. Leaving the terminal from the second floor gave me every chance of not being seen.

I walked slowly down the sidewalk of the departure level saying hi to everyone who appeared friendly. I did not try to hide. Hiding sometimes makes you stand out. I quickly slipped into the back seat of a cab that looked to have just dropped off a passenger. "How far will you take me?" I asked the startled driver. "I'm sorry to just jump in your cab. I am in a hurry," I offered as an apology.

"What's the address?" he inquired while reaching for the red flagged arm on his meter.

"I need to go to Moorpark."

"Could be costly," he said with a raised eyebrow.

"I'll double it if you don't call it in." The comment caused him to swivel around in his seat and give me a good once over. Before he asked anything, I shot him my best cheating husband grin and offered, "There's a PI looking for me. I may have been in Hawaii with someone who...wasn't my wife." My explanation was met with an approving smile.

"I'll need an address," he blurted.

"Give me time to dig it out, but go north on the 405 and I'll have it before you hit the 101." I honestly didn't know what to tell him. I couldn't go home and the office was out as well. I knew I had at least fifteen minutes before we reached one of the main arteries in Southern California.

Sitting back in the cab, I watched as we zipped by the hotels that lined Century Boulevard. Traffic was light, and inwardly I thanked the cabbie for getting me away from the airport quickly.

Suddenly, a staticky call over the radio heightened my attention. His beady eyes fixated on me through the rearview mirror while he spoke into the handset.

No! I thought to myself. I was being paranoid. A staticky call doesn't make my cabbie a killer. Whatever is happening cannot have this type of reach. My cabbie must be sizing me up, perhaps how to play me for a better tip.

But that's not what this is, that's not what this is by a long shot. I listened intently, I was able to pick out some words, however they were not English or Spanish. I couldn't place them until he spoke. They were French, a language I hadn't spoken for years, but the words were 'take him,' *Fuck!* I inwardly screamed. He slowed to make the 405 south transition. It was the correct highway, but the wrong direction. I was screwed.

I felt the sudden acceleration and thought, *it's now or never*! I leaned forward and wrapped my right arm around his neck. He didn't expect it; it was a clean grab. I locked my hands together, laid back in the seat...and pulled. He grabbed for my arm and sent several wild blows back towards me. It was futile. I held on, my life depended on it. The car careened left and right, but all I heard was the gurgling of a dying man. After what seemed an eternity, I moved forward, using his throat to pull myself up. I planted my head into the back of his seat, and squeezed. We were going to crash; he would never feel it.

Blaring horns screamed into my consciousness and were followed by a slamming, sudden lurching into the air. I flew forward and jammed my head into the roof, then felt the cab list left and smash onto the ground. The car continued to slide, slowly coming to a grinding stop. With tires still spinning the radiator blew, sending scalding hot water and steam out across the highway. My left arm was trapped in the folded metal of the driver's door. With a slight twist, I slowly raked my arm across the shattered glass, pulling it free.

I threw myself over the seat, ripped the cabbie's identification from the dash and compared the picture to my driver. They didn't match. I was an idiot.

"Are you okay?"

The muffled question came from somewhere outside behind the car.

"I'm okay!" I yelled. I smelled gas, a lot of gas. "Can you help me get out of here?!" The fumes started to burn my eyes and throat. "Hey, be careful out there. I think there's a gas leak."

Someone jumped on the side of the car, wrenched open the door, and yelled, "Can you make it out yourself?"

I turned around, pushed off of the driver's side, and stuck my legs out over the car's door frame. I used the seat to push myself out while several people grabbed my legs, and pulled me from the cab. Two men propped me up from each shoulder and walked quickly away from the wreck. They leaned me against one of the cars that had stopped for the crash. Minutes later, flashing lights filled the small area of parked cars that the good Samaritans had pulled together when they stopped to help. Two men kept their hands on my arms to keep me upright. I must have passed out, because when I regained consciousness, my stretcher was being jostled out of an ambulance.

* * *

My gurney was pushed up against a wall with four other patients waiting for a room. I never wish harm on most folks; however, I was happy to see a full emergency room. With this much activity it would be easy to slip out.

According to the paramedic, I had been given a low priority as I was only there for observation. After he left, I propped myself up on my elbows and surveyed my surroundings. Fortunately for me, it was busy. I pushed off the thin blue pad and up over the railing. After another quick look, I headed straight for the door I had come in, slipped past a sobbing crowd, and walked out into the dark.

It was funny; all I could think about was the safe deposit box. I was fixated on it. I had to get a look inside. I knew I could be putting Jessica at great risk.

There was no other way, I needed a woman I could trust, one that wouldn't fold at the last minute.

Oh, I know what you are thinking, *your client is dead, why worry about it, take the ten thousand and be happy*. I couldn't. I took the job and I was determined to finish it. If they hadn't tried to kill me, maybe things would be different. Maybe I'd be able to let it go.

11

After I walked out of the hospital, I found a place to hold up, a twenty-four-hour International House of Pancakes restaurant.

There I sat, trying not to stare at everyone who walked in.

However, as I was walking the streets searching for a place to hide, I made my first phone call and it was to Jessica. "Any luck with the wig?" I asked. I decided not to tell her what had happened with the cab driver.

"Got it yesterday after you called."

"Good, good. You are taller than the woman you're replacing, so wear flats. I'll need a picture of you wearing the wig in front of a white background and I need it fast."

"And there's no risk of the woman suddenly making an appearance when we are at the bank?"

It was a good question, and I was a bit hesitant to tell her, but Jessica doesn't spook easily, so I just said it. "My client is dead."

"Elizabeth Tully is dead?!"

"Ended up floating in the Ala Wai Canal in Waikiki."

"Jesus Richard!"

"Whatever is in that safe deposit box got her killed. I also believe it's what sent those murderers after us."

"What's your plan?"

"I want to be at the bank at eleven forty-five, about fifteen minutes before noon. I want to catch them close to lunch."

"I'll get this photo to you in a few minutes, then I'll wait for your call."

* * *

I walked into the restaurant holding my phone to my face as if on a call, it provided the concealment I needed. I sat at an inner table away from the window, but close the restroom, and the back door.

I knew I would be there for a while so I ordered the all-important, black coffee. I followed it with eggs, toast and a pile of meat.

Halfway through my meal, I received a text from Jessica. *Picture emailed*. I accessed my email account and quickly forwarded Jessica's picture and the photograph of Elizabeth Tully's driver's license to an acquaintance. I waited for ten minutes and then placed my second call.

"Marcus."

"Richard! So good to hear from you."

"I sent you something that needs your attention. And Marcus, I need it quick."

"I'll take a look."

His 'I'll take a look' was telling me he had already seen the email and was working on it. He'd replace Elizabeth Tully's California driver's license photograph with the one I received from Jessica. His work is so precise I knew the DMV would have trouble determining it was counterfeit. Yeah, I have a guy for this kind of thing.

One hour later, I received a call from Marcus. The license had been made and was ready for pick up. Two hours later, I left and pulled an all-nighter at several other twenty-four-hour restaurants. Then at eight in the morning I called Jessica.

"Ready?" she asked

"I am, but I have transportation issues. I'm south of you, not far really, just off the 405 close to Los Angeles International airport. I'll text you the address. We'll need to make a stop. Then we'll head to the bank.

"I'll leave in five."

"And Jess...thanks."

After Jessica picked me up, we made a stop at a park two blocks from Marcus's house. As I exited her car and closed the door, I said, "Wait here." I stepped onto the jogging path and walked deeper into the park. I stopped a man and politely asked him about his dog. I knelt, and with both hands ruffled the fur on his pup's head and ears. Then I pulled a small envelope from under his collar and slipped it in my pocket.

Ten minutes later, as we drove out of the neighborhood, I pulled Jessica's hot-off-the-press, California driver's license from the envelope and exclaimed, "Here you are." It was perfect. Tully's original license was two years old, and the one I was holding in my hand looked to be the same age. Next stop, the bank.

* * *

"Okay, how do we play this?"

Jessica asked the question I had known was coming. It was possible we were heading into a trap, and that was what worried me the most. I thought about it longer than I should have, and eventually I said, "I think it's best if you go in alone. Tell them you need to get into your safe deposit box and that it will only take a few minutes. Have your driver's license out and ready. It's lunch time, so they're not going to want to wait around. Don't take the time to look at whatever's in the box. Grab it all and get out of there. I'll move over to the driver's seat." Jessica stepped from the pushed open door. Before she closed it, I added, "Remember, you're the wife of the bank's president. Most of them probably have never met you, but a little attitude is expected, so play the part."

She chuckled. "Attitude? I think I can find some of that."

A dozen more questions ran through my mind. I was ready to tell Jessica about the cab driver, but then thought better of it.

Fifteen minutes after Jessica walked through the doorway, she returned holding a thick manila envelope in her hand. After closing the car door, she said, "Let's go". A few long seconds later, she added, "That was too easy."

Too easy didn't give me a warm and fuzzy. I needed to get a look in that envelope and soon.

I pulled away from the curb, headed straight for the highway, and shot Jessica a quick look. "Okay, let's get a peek at that file." From the corner of my eye, I watched her remove the stack of mix-matched papers from the envelope. I wanted to pull over and rifle through the pile myself, but I would get yelled at, and probably an elbow in the gut.

"Interesting," she finally said through a long sigh. Then she offered, "There is a reoccurring name; it's almost the theme of the stack." She continued to flip through the pages.

After what seemed like an hour, I impatiently asked, "And!" When she chuckled, I knew she was screwing with me.

"Larry McDonald," she finally said. "Ever hear of him?"

I searched my old dusty memory for a few long seconds. "No... never heard of him." I had just made the transition from highway 405 onto the 101 when my partner spit,

"Holy shit!" She had flipped a sheet of paper over, rubbed her finger on what looked like the signature line, and exclaimed, "Son of a bitch!"

Normally, Jessica reserves her sailor mouth for the bars. I've laughed so hard listening to her string together profanities that it had brought tears to my eyes, but this was different.

With her index finger, she again rubbed over the signature line from the back of the document. Finally, she exclaimed, "I can feel this signature, this is an original document, not a copy."

"So what?" I asked. "I have plenty of originally signed docs. What aren't you telling me?"

Looking at me with a half-grin, she shook the paper and said, "But do you have one signed by Ronald Reagan?"

12

"**R**onald Reagan, like President Ronald Reagan?"

"The one and only," she blurted.

"Well, that trumps my signed Steve McQueen poster." Twisting in her seat to face me, she continued to thumb through the documents, occasionally stopping to review a sheet. Minutes that seemed to turn into hours ticked by. Finally with an almost unrecognizable voice, and a look I had never seen from her, she gasped.

"Oh my God Dick! Oh my God! No...this can't be...no!"

I glanced over. She clutched the Reagan document and appeared lost in a gaze through the front windshield. She slowly looked at me through drenched eyes, tears streaming down her cheeks. "Jesus Christ, Jessica, what is it?"

"Pull over!" she blurted, "pull over!"

I stabbed my car into the next off-ramp, crossed over Burbank Boulevard, pulled into the Balboa Sports Center, and shifted the car into park harder than I should have. "Now, do you mind telling me what you found?" She didn't answer, but handed me three pages from her stack.

It had taken several long seconds to focus on what I had just been handed, and when I did, I studied them intently, flipping back and forth amongst the three. Finally, in a low, slow voice I heard myself say, "Holy shit!" In my hand were documents that could get us both killed. I looked up and outside of the car, assuring we were still alone. Jessica wiped her eyes and said,

"I don't know why I can't stop crying."

But I knew. The admiration she felt for President Ronald Reagan had just been shattered.

I reached over and slowly took the remaining pages from my passenger's hands. She gave them up freely, leaned forward, and began searching the glove box for something to wipe her face.

I took my time, and studied the pages meticulously, bouncing back and forth between unfamiliar names. I did my best to remember each person's role in what I was reading.

And before I go any further, I have to tell you. Over my career, I have held many secrets, and at times, top secret documents. I have been responsible for keeping safe knowledge of United States troop movements, insider trading, corporate espionage and, yes, husbands' and wives' extra-marital affairs. This was different, on a level I thought I'd never see.

I recognized a name from the Los Angeles Police Department's Public Disorder Intelligence Division. LAPD's Lieutenant Tom Sidedecker's name resonated in the recesses of my aged mind. I stared at his name trying to recall if I had actually met him or had just heard the name. However, I moved on, picking up another sheet of paper, but for some reason I couldn't put the Reagan document down. I felt conflicted. I was afraid to let it go and terrified to have it.

Another sheet, another name, Jay Paul, a detective with the LAPD. Who the hell was that? And why in nineteen eighty-three did an organization called the Western Goals Foundation pay his wife thirty thousand dollars a year to feed a huge batch of files into a computer in their garage. A few more lines and I hit pay dirt. "This is it! This," I said while nodding towards the Jay Paul paper, "is why our fortieth president penned this," I added, holding up the Reagan document.

Through a few lingering sniffles, Jessica whispered, "It was his death warrant."

Typed on White House stationery and signed by our fortieth president was the following: General Secretary, Yuri Andropov, the usefulness of Senator Larry McDonald has run its course. As agreed by the nation's state elimination program, as per presidential decree, is authorized by the

Convention. An overseas trip has been planned for Senator McDonald. Those details and approval will be forwarded via the Convention.

I read the document aloud, then to myself, not believing the words. However, there they were. I understood how Jessica felt. Although tears were not in my forecast, a deep sadness overtook me. There was no mistaking if it were a copy. It had been written on White House stationary; a beautifully embossed seal of the president adorned the top center of the page. I flipped over the paper and traced the indentation the signer's pen had made. I rubbed over the president's signature for the fifth time.

In my right hand I held what I had been calling the Reagan document. It authorized the killing of a senator. I was holding 'the why' in my other hand. The files that, Jay Paul was about to turn over to investigators had tied the senator to what he had been collecting over the years, of then California Governor Ronald Reagan.

According to what I had been reading, his testimony would not only severely damage Reagan, but the Reagan document would expose the Convention.

I turned to Jessica, nodded toward her smart phone, and instructed her to search for Senator Larry McDonald. I also needed to know more about the LAPD's Public Disorder Intelligence Division, Lieutenant Tom Sidedecker and piece together the

Convention. A call to my friend Shawn Vanderwerff was in the cards.

I punched in Shawn's number and waited. I hung up when it went to message. I tried again, and after several attempts, he finally answered.

"Mr. Maxim."

"Mr. Maxim?" I questioned. Suddenly, the space between Shawn and I felt cold.

"Do you realize everyone is looking for you?" he asked.

Now I started to pay attention to how long I was on the phone. Old habits, I guess. "And why is everyone looking for me?"

"It might have something to do with my dead cabbie," he sarcastically said.

"Yes, the accident I was involved in earlier. We crashed after the driver lost control of his car. He died?" I asked with a crooked grin.

"Of course, he did. The coroner dug a forty-five out of the back of his head."

"Wait! What! I shot who?" I spat.

"And there is an airport video of you getting into the cab," Shawn added.

As Shawn spoke, a dark sedan stopped along the curb in the opposing lane a short block away.

Looking over at Jessica, I motioned towards the new arrival.

"I found him, I found Larry McDonald," Jessica quietly uttered before turning to observe the sedan.

"Might be a good idea for you to drop by the precinct," Shawn said.

"Shawn, I just returned from Hawaii. I don't have my gun for Christ's sake!"

"As I remember, it's a forty-five," Shawn evenly countered.

"Damn it Shawn, I didn't shoot anyone!" I glanced over at Jessica who was giving me a worried look. Out of instinct, I patted under my left arm, knowing I wasn't going to feel my holstered handgun.

I sat quietly staring at the sedan, pressing the phone tight to my ear, angry that my friend was questioning me. Then something occurred to me. "Do you have something to write with?" I asked.

"No, not on me. My note pad is in my jacket pocket which is hanging over my desk chair...Was that a trick question?" he quipped.

"My guess is, since it had taken you awhile to answer this call you walked out of whatever room you were in."

After a long pause, he said. "Perhaps I wanted to give you the benefit of the doubt."

Or warn me, I thought. I pressed him a little further. "What do you know about LA's Department of Public Disorder and Intelligence Division and a Lieutenant Tom Sidedecker?"

"The PDID, that went down before my time, but it is still very fresh in everyone's memory. They were disbanded in the early eighties, something about spying on law-abiding citizens. If memory serves, I believe there was a lawsuit, and a payout, somewhere north of two million dollars."

"And Lieutenant Tom Sidedecker?" I prodded.

After a long silence, he answered, "No, doesn't ring a bell."

"Hey, can you take down this license plate number?"

"Trouble?"

"Not sure! A sedan pulled along the curb up from us, and no one has gotten out yet. He's just sitting there."

"Where are you, Dick?"

"Now who has the trick question?"

"My cell phone is on speaker. I'll enter the digits from the license plate into it. That'll do for now."

I held my fingers in a binocular shape around my eye, then pointed to the glove box for Jessica to retrieve hers. Just like the movies, all PIs have binoculars and a gun in their glove box. Well, except for the gun; that's just in books and movies. She handed me her glasses, and I studied the license plate's number and letters, 1MSTFSR, trying to turn them into a meaning. "Okay, here we go," I said into the phone. "The number one followed by Mike Sierra Tango Foxtrot Sierra Romeo." I handed the binoculars to Jessica and asked, "Can you make anything out of that?"

She took the glasses, and after a few long seconds, she shook her head and said, "Sure can't."

Shawn repeated the plate back to me and said, "Okay let me see what I can find."

"It might not be anything detective."

"But it might, Dick,' he answered, and ended the call.

Seconds after my phone fell silent, the door of the sedan opened.

13

"**W**hat the hell!" I said under my breath, but loud enough for Jessica to look up and ask,

"Who is that?"

I glanced her way. "That's the guy who materialized in my office the night I took this case. Came through a locked door, quiet as smoke through a keyhole." My partner gave me a quick look, and by the way her lips had curled up into a smirk, I could tell she appreciated my saying."

After a few long seconds, she offered, "he's ex-military," then added, "no, not military. He's a fed."

"A walking piece of the puzzle," I said in a low voice. *And just where do you fit?* I wondered. We both watched him walk across the street, favoring Jessica's side of the car. He stopped in front of her door. I knew the question was coming, so I said, "Put the window down. Let's see what he wants." She pressed the button, and the window disappeared into the door frame.

"Ms. Sleeman, I presume." When he offered her his paw, she took it and gave it a firm shake. Then he added, "Mr. Maxim, I hear you had an interesting time in Hawaii."

"My time in Hawaii was...different, but I'm afraid you have us at a disadvantage. Much like the other night, I didn't catch your name."

"My name is not important. What is important is that envelope you have."

I looked at the papers that were lying on our laps and asked, "Do you know what these are?"

"No, no, I do not." He answered sounding bewildered. "However." He continued, "I do believe that folder is what I have been searching for. Apparently, it was locked in the safe deposit box Ms. Sleeman just cleaned out."

"And now it's ours...finders keepers." I shot back sarcastically. However, now I knew he was a fed. I knew because we were both still alive.

"Mr. Maxim, this is not a game. Your client's husband took possession of that box. It had information stored in it that he was never to see. It's true I do not know exactly what that is, but I do know it has already gotten several people killed. You two could be next."

"I don't scare easily," I replied.

"No, I suppose you don't, Mr. Maxim."

"It appears we are at a stalemate," I offered.

"No, we really aren't." he said while pulling back his suit jacket. The black semi-automatic handgun sat high on his hip in a leather holster. I instantly recognized it as a Glock twenty-three.

"He's right!" Jessica added, holding up her phone, pushing past the stranger's veiled threat. "This Senator, Larry McDonald, died in a plane crash in nineteen eighty-three. Actually, it reads that the commercial airline he was traveling in was shot down by a Soviet interceptor while in route to a meeting in South Korea, Seoul to be exact. Twenty-three crew members and all two hundred forty-six passengers were killed."

"Not just killed." I held up the Reagan document and uttered, "but murdered." *Jesus Christ,* I thought. Could a president have a person killed along with whomever else just happened to be around them? The question was not only could he, but would he?

"Mr. Maxim, I'm trying to root out certain... unknown organizations."

Our visitor's comment shook me from my thoughts. He continued,

"Our paths crossed because you have information I need in order to do that."

My mind wandered for a moment, then I pushed open the car's door and stepped from it. I looked at the big man, and with a tilt of my head I motioned to the rear of the car. As we walked back, I heard the passenger door open, and seconds later a stern voice was taking me to task.

"If you think you are not including me, you're crazier than a hoot owl."

Jessica normally doesn't scold me, but when she does, she occasionally uses one of my sayings, which I thought was a clear sign that I was rubbing off on her. Inwardly, I smiled.

Jessica and I squared off with the fed. She gathered the papers that had been laid around the car and stuffed them in the envelope she held in her hand. I still clutched the Reagan document. "Unknown organizations?" I spouted. "Is that fancy for secret societies?" The moment I asked the question, Jessica let out a screech, and another loud cry followed what sounded like a muffled gunshot, no, there were two gun shots. Several slugs pounded into Jessica's car; pieces of shrapnel raked across the back of my hand. The three of us scrambled around to the front of the car. I looked back to check Jessica and I noticed blood was running down her right arm. I peered over the hood; blood was splattered over the back of the car.

"I'll cover you, move her to my car," the stranger barked.

He pulled the Glock from his holster with lightning speed, not hesitating to press off several rounds at a fleeing van. The pistol spat shell casings all over the road. The fed went from adversary to guardian in the press of a trigger. I pulled Jessica away from the car and rushed her across the street. The sleeve of her right arm and the side of her shirt were soaked with blood. I read the pain in her twisted face and pursed lips. I removed a handkerchief from my pocket and wrapped it around her arm, keeping pressure on the wound. Then I looked back across the street. The fed appeared to be favoring his right side. With his left hand, he pulled his jacket away and glanced at what I was sure was a bullet hole. He, too, had been shot. And I realized then that the blood all over the back of the car was his.

I felt naked without my gun. In fact, I felt ridiculous not having it. I questioned my reasoning for leaving it behind, but I had intended for my Hawaii trip to be low key. I had wanted no undue attention that checking a firearm would bring. Now I saw the flaw in my thinking.

The big man stood in the open. He lowered his gun while watching the van race off. He did a quick three-sixty and returned his gaze to our attackers until they were out of sight. "We're not going after them?" I asked.

"No. They're just lackeys sent to do someone else's dirty work. How is she?" he asked, nodding at Jessica.

I tilted my head toward her arm and said, "This is going to hurt." I pulled the blood-soaked handkerchief I was using to apply pressure to her arm away from her shirt, and picked pieces of shirt fabric out of her arm with my fingers. "It's not that bad." I lied. She was missing a chunk of bicep.

As if on cue, a few minutes after this type of trauma, a person's brain catches up to the pain. As I watched the color drain from her face, I softly asked, "Hey! Are you okay? You're a bit pale."

"Oh, I'm just fine damn it. Jesus, Dick, this hurts like hell!"

The tears welling in her strained eyes told me she was holding back the floodgates.

As the fed approached, I offered, "The bullet traveled between her arm and body, nicking her arm."

He gave me a questioning look, then added, "She was lucky."

Through several shaky breaths, Jessica countered. "I don't feel lucky."

"Six inches to the left and there would have been no reason for Dick here to drag you across the street. That first shot was for you. Someone wants you dead."

After the fed glanced around the area, he continued,

"I figure we have another minute before this place is crawling with cops." After a quick nod towards Jessica, he added, "Get her some help."

"And you?" I asked, looking at his jacket as if I could see the bloodied shirt.

"I'll be fine. It's just a flesh wound, and besides, I've been shot before."

"Shot before or not," I blurted, "it freakin' hurts." I was annoyed at him for being so nonchalant about being shot. Who was this guy?

I looked down at the Reagan document I still held in my hand and over at the folder Jessica still held in hers. Super fed or not, he wasn't getting the papers until I was ready to hand them over.

"I'm sure our paths will cross again." He said with a nod towards the folder.

I nodded my agreement, then rushed Jessica back across the street and into her car. I pulled the seat belt over her chest and snapped the silver catch into the lock. "Keep pressure on the handkerchief." It wasn't enough to control the bleeding. I knew she needed to see a doctor.

Seconds after I slipped into the driver's seat, Jessica said,

"I've never been shot before."

For some reason Jessica's comment made me smile. Perhaps it was the relief I felt, relieved my friend wasn't dead.

* * *

I couldn't stop the thoughts from swirling around my head as I shifted into drive, pressed the gas pedal, and launched the car up the on-ramp and onto the highway. I was headed north to see the best person who could help my passenger, my pal Doctor Mak.

Why do I keep seeing the stranger? Was that bullet really meant for Jess? Was someone watching the bank? Was this all set up because my client had made a phone call?

And who the hell shot my driver!?

14

Thirty minutes later, I pulled the car into Mak's driveway. Before sliding out of the car, I punched the seat belt release for Jessica's seat belt. Thirty minutes is a long time to be in pain, and Jessica's color and slurred speech told me she was close to passing out. I was thankful to have help close by and even happier to see the good doctor open the side gate.

I pulled open the passenger door, carefully removed Jessica's seat belt, and helped her out of the car. I slipped my arm around her waist and propped her up using her left armpit. Jess weighed about a buck twenty-five soaking wet so when she leaned into me, I hardly noticed.

The doctor walked through the side gate and joined us at the car. The three of us walked around the house and entered through a side door. We set Jessica in a dentist chair that yours truly had purchased after several late-night visits with clients.

I called Mak about ten miles south of the house and now I couldn't be happier to have my friend in a doctor's care.

"Doc, this is Jessica Sleeman. Jessica, this is Doctor Lorran Makenzie."

"You brought me to a dentist?" Jess asked through a strained voice.

Makenzie laughed and offered, "The chair? That's compliments of your friend here. Dick has a habit of showing up needing after-hour's assistance."

"I thought it might be a good idea to make the after-hours clients a bit more comfortable," I added. Okay, the after-hours client was me, but that's a story for another time.

Mak stuck a hypodermic needle into Jessica's arm. With a glance in my direction, she said. "This will put her under." Then added, "and speaking of late-night visitors, how's your leg?"

"It's fine." I answered, instinctively rubbing my thigh. The slice had been deep and five stitches long. I nodded towards Jessica and asked, "Is there anything I can do to help?" I had to ask, but already I knew the answer. Makenzie shook her head and then nodded towards a chair across the room, but before I sit, I needed to return to the car. "I'll be right back," I said, and then quickly left the house, went to the car, and grabbed the manila envelope. I wasn't leaving it unattended any longer than needed. I paused when I held the Reagan document, still not believing what

I had been reading. I found myself being a bit more careful with it as I returned it to the envelope.

Quietly, I walked back into the house and eased myself into a black, soft leather chair. I set the envelope on my lap and turned my attention to the two women who had been so involved in my life. I found it curious they had never met.

*   *   *

I met Doctor Lorran Makenzie while at the VA hospital years ago and forged a lasting friendship. We got off to a rocky start, and I quickly found she was a force to be reckoned with.

I was there to pick up my meds. I thought it was going to be a routine visit, but a poking and prodding session ensued.

When I arrived at the hospital, I went directly to the pharmacy. However, a pharmacy tech pointed to an open door of an exam room and instructed me to wait for Doc Mak. I did just that. I went into the exam room and chose to sit on a small black rolling chair instead of the exam table with it's paper covered thin black pad.

There I waited until there was a knock at the door. I barked an acknowledgement and the door slowly opened. In walked a woman just under five five. Her long brown hair flowed over a thin frame. "I expected a man," I barked. I figured I'd show her who the boss was right from the start. "I'm here for my blood pressure meds and nothing else." She pointed to the table and said,

"Sit on the end and dangle your legs. This will be quick."

Only it wasn't quick, after she smacked me a few times on the knee with that godawful hammer, she proceeded to poke and prod me and drill me with twenty questions. To top it off, I found myself bent over the exam table, with my elbows firmly implanted in its thin mattress, for a long overdue prostate check. Her fingers weren't large, but they didn't need to be.

I had just finished pulling myself back together and heard, 'here, take this,' as she handed me a slip of paper. 'It's for the lab. I'll need urine and some blood work.' I started to protest, but thought better of it, thinking my mouth may have been what had gotten me into this. And then it happened... She turned to wash her hands and, in the reflection of the stainless-steel paper towel dispenser, I saw the corners of her lips turn into a smile. 'I'll see you next week when we get the results back.' She said, shaking the water from her hands into the sink. When she faced me, the smile was gone. I returned a slight grin and a slow suspicious nod. "I'll see ya next week, Doc."

As I took a step through the doorway, she added, "Oh, Mr. Maxim, my dad says hi."

I froze while her words, *my dad says hi*, circled my gray matter. Makenzie, Makenzie. I said her name over and over. Quickly, I thought of past clients. Nothing, damn it! I stepped back through the doorway and asked, "Your dad is who?"

'Colonel Makenzie' came the reply. Still nothing. I instantly thought back to my Vietnam days, but the name still had no meaning.

"I can tell from that blank look that you don't remember the guy that flew you around, how did he put it, that godawful country."

"I'm sorry, Doc. I don't know your dad." She smiled and said,

"You didn't know Chief Warrant Officer Hatchet?"

"Oh my God! You're Hatchet's daughter?" Yeah, I was taken aback. Hatchet was our helicopter pilot from the 25th Infantry Division. He was assigned to our group in Vietnam. Pilots not only carried their sidearm across their chest, but many carried knives tied to their thighs. Not our guy. He had one of the fiercest looking hatchets I had ever seen strapped to him, earning him his nickname.

Our Huey was a "Slick" and Hatchet flew it so low and fast foliage was often wedged in our skids. To save weight it was not fitted with external weapons. We only had our door gunner and crew chief manning their M60 machine guns and our crazy pilot with his hatchet strapped upside down on his leg.

I was flooded with memories and admittedly I felt emotional. For a moment I heard those forty-eight-foot blades thumping the air. I looked up at the doc, searching her face for our pilot. More memories came rushing back. I felt the corners of my eyes fill with water, and I started to sweat. *No!* I thought. I pushed my growing anxiety down. The night terrors I had experienced were long gone... or were they?

"Are you okay?" she asked.

"I'm fine." It's what a vet tells someone who has no idea what they had been through. Like I said, I had seen things no man should ever see. Suddenly, I realized I was sitting on the edge of the exam table. "I'm sorry I forgot your dad's last name. He was always John Hatchet to us. I loved that guy. Kept us out of trouble." I shelved the memories and asked, "So, he retired a Colonel?" 'Full bird.' She offered. I smiled, stood, walked over to Makenzie, and gave her a bear hug. "Give that to your dad the next time you see him. But how in the world did you connect the two of us?"

"My dad rarely spoke of the war. When he did, it was always about the three men he provided taxi service for."

"Taxi service," I said with a chuckle.

"Well, that's what he called it. He knew you were in the LA area, always meant to look you up. Said if I ever ran into you at the VA to say hi."

Now it was her turn. Her eyes glistened, and she fought hard to hold back the flood gates.

Her voice broke when she said, 'Cancer took him a few years ago.' I leaned in and gave her another hug, only this one seemed to connect us. We stood in the middle of the small room and cried. Both for the loss of her dad, and for me, me for a war I fought in my head long after it was over.

I stepped back, held out my hand, and said, "Doctor, allow me a better introduction. I'm Dick Maxim." She grabbed it with both hands, gave it a tight squeeze, and said,

"Mr. Maxim, I'm Lorran Makenzie. I can't tell you how nice it is to meet you."

"Doc, I'm a private investigator now. If there's anything you ever need, don't hesitate to call." With that said, I flipped out my business card and added, "I'm sure sorry I never reconnected with your dad. What a great guy. He was able to get us out of some tight spots." Before the waterworks started, I turned towards the doorway, but stopped short and asked. "So, the prostate check, was that your dad's idea?"

"No, that was all me. It was payback."

"Payback!?" I prodded.

"For laughing at my dad when he was shot in the rear."

"He told you that was my fault?!" Inwardly, I laughed at the memory.

And that is how I met Hatchet's daughter, and she's been a good friend and a godsend for late-night visits. It's funny how life plays out.

* * *

Out of the blue, Lorran asked,

"I probably shouldn't know how Miss Sleeman ended up missing some of her bicep?"

It was a veiled question and only a veiled answer would do. "Do you want to know why your dad really got shot in his ass?"

"Okay, don't tell me. But, Dick, a gunshot!?"

I met her eyes, which glared from over the top of a thin pair of black glasses and said,

"I was hoping you wouldn't notice." I knew she would notice. I was hoping she wouldn't ask.

Finally, she looked away. It felt like my mother had just scolded me.

I watched her carefully wrap an oversized gauze dressing around Jessica's arm. I knew she was making a point. Pushing her wheeled chair with her foot, she rolled across the room and stopped at a closet. She retrieved a thick white towel and rolled it into a fluffy log. After gliding back to her patient, she lifted Jessica's arm and gently placed it under her bicep.

"Finished. Would you like my recommendation?"

"No!" I said harsher than I should have, which earned me another hard look.

I watched as she wiped down the tools of her trade and neatly placed them on shelves in her tabletop autoclave. She closed and locked the stainless-steel door, flipped up the power switch, and walked out of the room.

For a moment I stared at the machine, lost in its low hiss. My eyes burned, and I realized I couldn't remember what day it was. I broke my gaze and stared at the floor, thinking, *Sunday? No, no today is Monday.* I was tired and fatigue causes you to do dumb things.

15

What was my next move? I had a signed document by a former president authorizing the assassination of an American citizen. You know as well as I do, my client is dead and there are people trying to kill me. And why shoot the cab driver? Was I being set up so the police could help whomever look for me? And why the hell hadn't I retrieved my gun?

I looked over at Jessica, then pushed myself up from the chair at the same time Makenzie walked back into the room. I quietly asked, "Mind if I run off for a few minutes?" I smiled when she looked down at two dripping-wet bottles of beer she held in her hand. I glanced at them and said, "Hold that thought. I'll be right back." My next move was to retrieve my gun. Fortunately, I didn't live far from the doc.

I have to be honest; it was hard leaving that chair and the beer would have been a nice precursor to some much-needed sleep. However, I really wanted my gun.

Fifteen minutes later, I pulled along the curb three blocks from my house. I knew a stroll would be less conspicuous. As I walked towards my house, a thought pushed itself up through my subconscious: the Reagan document. In it, the president wrote '*the usefulness of Senator Larry McDonald has run its course. As agreed by our two nation's state elimination, as per presidential decree, is authorized by the Convention.*'

The Convention... what was that, or... who was that?

Over the years, I have had trusted sources whisper *secret societies* in my ear. Could Reagan have been part of one? Did the senator try to have Reagan killed in eighty-one? Or was his assassination attempt a message? Was he marked by the *Convention*?

No, that's not right, not the Convention. Reagan was connected with them in eighty-three when he ordered the killing of MacDonald. Was the convention something you join? What was I missing? The senator was subpoenaed by the Los Angeles grand jury. What did he really have on Reagan? Whatever it was, it was enough to not only get himself killed, but two hundred and sixty-eight innocent folks along with him.

I stopped down the street from my house, knelt down adjacent to a large tree, and fiddled with my shoelaces. I tried not to draw much attention. A black-and-white, two dark sedans, and a black SUV were parked in front of my humble abode. Shawn was right. I was being looked for.

I should have thrown Mrs. Elizabeth Tully out of my office at the first opportunity. I know, a dame with long legs can cause a man to do dumb things.

Experience only counts if you trust your gut, and my gut said it was time to leave.

I stood, then suddenly, in an even tone, a familiar voice resonated in my ears. 'I see you came back for your gun.' As I turned around my face flushed with anger. Not necessarily at the large man standing in front of me, no, I was angry with myself. How the hell could he have snuck up behind me? And there it was, my forty-five, dangling from its trigger guard around the thick finger of the fed.

I stared at him, seeing the gun in my periphery. From behind his back, he pulled my holster and offered it with a crooked smile. Once I had it in place, he grabbed the gun by its frame and handed it to me. I eased the slide back and checked for a round. Seeing one, I removed the magazine and stuck it in my pocket. Then I pulled back the slide, ejected the cartridge in the palm of my hand, and then pushed up the slide lock. Instinctively I dropped the round in my pocket and from the magazine I thumbed out a new cartridge and slid it in the chamber and eased the slide forward.

Here's what I learned in Nam: just because someone hands you a gun that was loaded, doesn't mean that it is still loaded, especially someone you don't know.

Once I had my gun secured in its holster, I looked up at the man and asked, "How long have you been here?"

"Just arrived. I had your 1911 when we met earlier. Thought I'd keep it a little longer."

"What made you give it back?"

"Consider it a peace offering. And now we need to go."

I nodded my head in agreement and as we walked away, I asked, "Did you shoot the cab driver?"

'I assumed he was already dead,' he answered. I flashed him a questioning look and quickly he added,

"Because if I had been in the back seat, that's how I would've handled it."

I was starting to like this guy.

One block away, he broke the silence. "You and I have to come to some sort of agreement."

And for some reason that was when it hit me. This had nothing to do with Reagan, Senator MacDonald, or the Tullys for that matter. I was thrown by having a document signed by Reagan. This had everything to do with information. Information was power and whoever held this document had the power.

I glanced over my shoulder to check our six, then stopped. "I know why you are interested in what I have. It hit me a second ago."

He took another step, stopped, turned, and, as if he were attending a funeral, said. "Mr. Maxim, our country is in danger, in danger of hidden forces, forces I'm trying to root out. Until we get a president and members of congress with the balls to upset the apple cart, I'm afraid our democracy won't make it another twenty years. Not long ago, I went up against what I believed was a secret society. Unfortunately, some of its members may have been killed."

May have been killed, I thought. *And who may have killed them?* As I digested the information, I started feeling sick to my stomach. And I was sure he could see the concern that no doubt registered on my face.

"Instead of our government focusing on what the constitution requires, national defense, they and other factions, choose other wars. It's an economic war, it's a war of subversion, it's a war of espionage, it's a war of ideas, it's a war of terrorism, and it's a war of infiltration." He turned, took a few more paces, stopped, and added, "The erosion of American sovereignty, and her moral compass, is their true goal, and guess what it's all about?"

"Money!" I blurted.

"It boils down to two things, want and need. Men want the money, but they need the power. That's it, simple greed. Some people can't be happy with the little things, hell they can't be happy with the big things. No, Mr. Maxim, they need it all, every bit of it. And they won't stop until they have it, or die trying to get it."

After a slight pause the fed continued.

"Do you know what the tenth commandment is, Mr. Maxim?"

"Not a clue," I answered.

"Thou shall not covet."

"Thy neighbor's wife," I added. "But religion? Now we are bringing religion into all of this?" I asked. He gave me a quick look and continued with,

"Thy neighbor's wife was never a part of the commandment. It was later added as a diversion, a distraction, if you will."

We walked for a minute and the fed continued.

"Thou shall not covet, thou shall not want, thou shall not desire, thou shall not yearn for, thou shall not crave."

"Okay, okay, I get it," I blurted.

"It's part of our moral decay and the man upstairs knew it."

I understood perfectly. It was no different than a man who has the perfect wife. If he sees a beautiful woman, he'll start to fantasize, then he will start to want. I saw it all the time.

The more he spoke, the more his intensity changed. I realized he needed the document more than I did. Besides, what the hell was I going to do with it? "I'll make you a deal," I offered. "Follow me back to my friend's house and I'll turn over what we have."

"In exchange for?"

With a backwards tilt of my head, I said, "Clearly, I'm being hunted. Help me and Miss Sleeman clear our names."

"Deal!" came the quick response.

We walked for a few minutes and the stranger asked, 'What is a lifetime?' I knew the question was rhetorical. I also felt that he didn't seem to be a person who shared much, so I waited.

"For each person, it's different. Some live a few short years, some thirty and some over one hundred years."

I could tell the fed had something on his mind, so I let him continue uninterrupted. I know, I'm a good listener.

"As kids, all we want to do is play outside, ride our bikes."

"And damn well better be home when the streetlights come on," I quickly added.

He lightly chuckled and continued.

"Unfortunately, some are groomed with what some are born with. A gene firmly attached to their genome. It's called greed. As we move through our lives, that gene grows stronger, especially if it is nourished. For some it is their environment, and that is where the grooming comes in. Eventually it becomes all consuming, and that brings us back to the want and need."

We walked for a few more minutes and then he asked.

"Streetlights? They had them when you were a kid?"

"As a matter of fact, my friend Ben Franklin was having them installed," I quipped.

"A history buff, I see. Democracy is two wolves and a lamb voting on what to have for lunch. Liberty is a well-armed lamb contesting the vote!"

"A Franklin quote!" I offered.

"He is one of my favorites. We owe him a lot."

"Well, at least we have something in common; we both seem to like Franklin."

"And guns, Mr. Maxim. I've seen your collection. It's modest, but well thought out."

My collection was modest? I've never thought of it as modest, but I'll take the *well thought out.*

We both made it back to our cars, and this time no one was shooting at us.

Twenty minutes later, we pulled our cars into Doc Makenzie's driveway. Minutes later, it became painfully clear that the women were gone, and the trail of blood told us they hadn't left willingly.

16

I followed the blood out of the house. After stepping through the back door, I spat. "I'll kill who's responsible for this." Just as I hit my boiling point, my phone rang. I quickly fished it out of my pocket. Jessica's name prominently appeared on the screen. I answered while holding the phone away from my ear.

"You know what we want, and tell Springfield to stay away."

The line went dead. Now I had a name. I looked at the fed and asked, "You Springfield?" Slowly, he nodded his head. He searched my eyes, like he was sizing me up, but I was in no mood for that shit. Suddenly, he held out his hand and said, 'Mark.' I took his paw and gave it a shake, then he offered,

"We need to find your friends."

He knelt down and removed what looked like a phone from his pocket. He ran his index finger through the wet blood that was splattered on the floor and smeared it across the screen from one corner to the next. I watched the odd behavior for a few torturous minutes. After his device buzzed, he removed a small package from his jacket pocket, tore open its cellophane wrapper, and removed what looked like an alcohol pad. After wiping the screen and his finger, he stood up.

What in God's name could he possibly be doing? I slid my phone into my pocket and walked into an adjacent room. Before I had left the doc's house, I had slipped the folder Jessica had snatched from the safe deposit box between two cushions of an overstuffed couch. I retrieved it, walked back out to the fed, handed it to him, and said, "Here. Here's my part of the bargain." Taking the folder, he took the few steps to a chair and sat down. I watched him open and riffle through the paperwork. He stopped and studied the document I knew would catch his attention. I could see the seal of the White House as he shuffled the pages around. Slowly, he removed the Reagan document. I watched him scan the sheet of paper.

Finally with a nod of his head, he said, "The Convention."

"That's what I was talking about while walking back to the cars." I was being patient; I was giving him time to sort through what I had already seen. Several long minutes passed. I felt I needed to hurry him along and so I added, "The Convention. That's what this is about."

"Mr. Maxim, I'm going to write a book, I'm going to call it, in walks a PI."

It was an odd statement, so I gave the fed an odd look. He pointed to an adjacent chair and, while holding up the envelope, he said,

"The contents of this will keep your friends alive. Have a seat."

I hesitantly took the few steps and sat down. I felt edgy. We weren't racing out of the house after the girls. The fed was killing me, my friends had been taken, and did I mention the blood? I started to protest, but what he said next surprised me.

"Eight months ago, I got wind of an organization that needed further scrutiny. I, well we, have been looking for evidence of a controlling organization. This organization could very well be this convention.

I thought for a moment and offered. "Mrs. Tully was key."

"*Is* key. Mr. Maxim, your client is not dead. Elizabeth Tully did not die in the canal."

"No!" I protested. "Her body was floating in the...!"

"No, that was not Elizabeth Tully."

"Then who for Christ's sake!" After a long pause, he uttered.

"Her sister Brenda, an unwitting accomplice in all of this, was lured to Hawaii by none other than Mrs. Tully, herself."

Instantly, I was taken back to the canal. I stared at the floor while watching a video play in my mind.

And there it was, a fanned-out detail that had escaped me. The body in the canal had shorter hair. "Elizabeth is... alive?" I hesitantly asked. "But how?" Springfield nodded towards the envelope and said,

"They had to get into that safe deposit box and couldn't risk being seen. Having you believe she was dead would force your hand. And I believe they killed two birds with one stone, got you to act and eliminated a problem. Brenda started asking questions."

The fed gave me an odd look and continued,

"And in walks a PI."

He paused for a long second and added,

"You, Mr. Maxim, were, in a word, played."

His absurd comment hit me hard. I had two dead bodies in my house, a dead cabby, and a floater to prove this was no normal, hey look over there while I steal your wallet, game.

"Maxim, you have no idea what these people will do. Take this, for example."

The fed held up the Reagan document and continued,

"As Mrs. Sleeman pointed out, flight double-o-seven was shot down by a Soviet interceptor, but what she didn't read was that the plane stopped in Fairbanks, Alaska, and a few key people got off. It continued onto Seoul with Senator McDonald, who was still onboard, and as you know, the plane never made it."

Springfield stuffed all the pages back into the envelope and added.

"They brought down a plane full of people to get one guy."

"Why not just shoot him? Why bring down an entire plane!?" I knew the question came out harsh, but none of it made sense. What Springfield said next told me clearly that he had been busy the last eight months.

"He was scheduled to deplane in Alaska, had a room booked at the Anchorage Grand Hotel."

The fed paused, and continued with,

"He also had a hunting trip set up, a little distraction before going onto Seoul, but he never got off the plane in Fairbanks."

"Something, or someone, spooked him." I offered.

"Yes, because what better way to eliminate a problem than with an Alaskan hunting accident."

After a long pause, Springfield added,

"Senator McDonald set up his own secret society and in fact was on the cusp of an expansion like no one had ever seen, but he didn't see the big picture. That big picture panicked when he outsmarted them and never got off the plane. However, he unwittingly sealed the fate of the passengers when he went onto Seoul."

"You keep mentioning Seoul. Why there? What was happening in South Korea?"

"The Heritage Foundation Defense Conference. But that's not why he was really there. He was there to set up the Heritage Foundation's Asian Studies Center.

The look on my face must have told the fed I was confused. It sounded like a noble cause.

"Are you familiar with think tanks?" he asked.

"Yeah, I hear about them from time to time."

"Do you know most think tanks operate as nonprofits under the Internal Revenue Code? They are not required to expose a list of their sponsors or donors."

After a long pause, he added,

"And now for the perfect crime. Ninety-two million dollars in donations from sixty-four foreign governments went into twenty-eight think tanks. They can dole out the money with impunity. The worst part: the press is tied into the think tanks and they have been for a while. And guess where it started... The Heritage Foundation's Asian Studies Center. It was the next phase of his plan, to control the press. Its purpose is to provide Asian journalists greater access to policymakers inside the Beltway. Washington correspondents from Japan, Taiwan, Korea, China, and other countries in the region get access to the strongest country on Planet Earth. Now sprinkle in highly paid lobbyists, invite key brethren reporters from the US, set up mirrors, add a little smoke, a lot of money funneled from the think tanks, and they'll report whatever you tell them to."

It was almost too much to believe. Could I trust someone I had just met? "There can't be a boogieman under every bed," I offered.

"No, Mr. Maxim. Some are women who break through your bedroom door in the middle of the night."

I thought for a moment and stated, "You were in the car behind my house. Why did you leave?"

"When I heard the shotgun blast, I knew you had a handle on it."

He offered a grin and continued with,

"And now for the very dark side of all of this, and to demonstrate how much power the press has, but more importantly how much power their puppet masters have, one month after the shoot down. The president of South Korea was the target of an assassination attempt."

"Yes, I vaguely remember that." I offered. The fed gave me a slight smile which looked out of character; he didn't seem to be someone who smiled.

"Yes, *vaguely* is the operative word, Mr. Maxim. Even though seventeen people died, and that includes four of his cabinet members, it was hardly reported. The press was already at work, but not reporting, suppressing, and we are talking only a month or so in. They were becoming agenda-driven, not truth-driven. The senator was intercepted because whoever set up the foundation was going to control the press."

"And the press controls what we see." I offered.

"Not only that, Mr. Maxim. They control how we see it. And we both know the end game."

I thought for a moment and asked, "Which is?"

"Whoever controls the media, controls the masses."

His comment wasn't an answer, but a hard statement.

How could all of this be planned, tracked, and funded on a global scale and what the hell had I gotten into? Unexpectedly, a phone buzzed. I watched Springfield pull one from his pocket. He turned it in a few directions while studying the screen. Finally, he said,

"Time to go."

We both stood. He handed me the manilla envelope and said,

"Put this someplace safe."

I walked into the other room and slipped it between the couch cushions. When I returned, he handed me his phone and asked, 'What's our fastest route?' I took his phone and quickly discovered it was different. At a glance, it looked like any smartphone, but after a closer look, I determined it was unlike any phone I had seen. A little heavier and slightly thicker. The screen glowed with a blue hue when viewed from any direction other than straight on. With a finger on the screen, I moved the image. The longitude and latitude coordinates around the image changed and scaled themselves when I used my thumb and forefinger to alter the size. I continued to move the image out until it was clear what I was looking at. I knew the answer, but asked, "Is this from a satellite?"

"Is it?" he countered.

He had access to a satellite. After working in intelligence during my Vietnam days, I knew the type of people who had space toys. Those people were spies, and not just regular spies. They were highly connected and trusted men and women of the alphabet soup. And now I knew who he was. Maybe it was his way of telling me without actually telling me. Springfield was part of one of the big five intelligence agencies. I didn't peg him as someone who sat behind a desk, so he wasn't part of the NRO (National Reconnaissance Office) or affiliated with the NSA (National Security Agency). I wasn't sure what the NGA (National Geospatial-Intelligence Agency) does. That group started after my Vietnam days. I thought they map. I knew this guy didn't sit and draw pictures all day. That left the CIA or the DIA. I squared with him and asked, "Central Intelligence or the Defense Intelligence Agency?"

His tone was flat when he answered.

"Well, I wouldn't work for the DIA."

A spook, great! I thought. This just kept getting better and better. I looked back at the device and said, "Now that we got that cleared up, head 101 north, exit Seaward Street, left over the highway, left on Pierpont, right on Shelburn." On the map, I viewed light green brackets affixed around a white roofed house sitting on the corner of Shelburn Lane on Ventura beach.

After I handed him back the device, he said,

"We'll take my car, yours is shot up."

17

I had been doing this line of work long enough to know I wouldn't get an answer, but as we drove north, I couldn't let a nagging detail go. "Mind telling me what the blood smear was all about?" My question had no effect on the fed. He simply continued to drive, occasionally checking his mirrors. I didn't press the question. If he wasn't going to tell me the first time, I was sure asking again would have the same outcome.

The trip north would take roughly twenty minutes, but until my friends were safe, I knew it would feel like an eternity. As we traveled north, the space between us felt odd, so I broke the silence with another question. "Did they really need to kill Elizabeth's sister?" This one he answered.

"Like I said, they had to get you to act, and act fast. Thinking Tully was dead would force your hand. These people know you; they knew what you would do. Mr. Maxim, they are ruthless."

I was very familiar with the beaches of Ventura. They are nestled in Southern California, and the mild climate draws beautiful women and cheating husbands to its shores. Over the years, I have investigated other nefarious activities, from the drug trade to missing women sold for sex. Springfield has his fancy gizmo, but I can navigate us around the tourists, and deep sand that has been blown over the narrow streets.

In route to Ventura, we exited the highway and performed zig zags through the small town of Camarillo. I was sure my driver was using the surface streets to check for any unwanted tails eventually reentering the highway.

Ten minutes later, we exited the 101 on the Seaward off-ramp and drove onto the lot of a corner gas station. He swung the car around and backed into an end parking space. The spy, yeah, I said spy, pulled his phone from his pocket, and as he removed it, I heard it vibrate. After looking at the screen and manipulating it with his fingers, he said,

"Your friends have been moved."

"Shit!" I blurted.

"No, that's a good thing." After a quick glance, he added, "Means they're still alive."

My hands were tied, but him telling me that was somewhat comforting. I watched him manipulate his device—I say device because I was sure it wasn't a phone. Looking out over the freeway, he said with a nod,

"Now we continue north."

I didn't like it; I didn't like it at all being this far out of control. I'm in a car with someone I hardly knew, involved in God knows what, chasing after friends who were taken against their will by, for lack of a better word, a shadow group. No, I didn't like it one damn bit.

We pulled back onto Seaward and accelerated down the on-ramp. The fed set the cruise control to seventy, checked all of the mirrors, and after another quick look at the device, settled back into the seat. The mood in the car felt...off. With his bunched together eyebrows and pursed lips, I could tell the fed was at odds with himself. Several quiet minutes later, he broke the silence with a peculiar statement.

"As long as there are virtuous men, what is done in the darkness will always come to light."

Who the hell talks like that? I thought for a moment, and the answer seemed simple... A virtuous man does.

"Mr. Maxim, do you know Elizabeth Tully's maiden name?"

Her maiden name... It was something I had never considered, so my answer was "No!"

'McDonough.' He firmly stated.

I thought for a moment, but the name meant nothing to me. "That is?" I asked.

"Elizabeth's father is William McDonough, president of the Federal Reserve Bank of New York. Well, former. He retired last year, but he keeps his hands in the banking world. Even easier that his daughter is married to Tully, a bank president. Now, let's talk about her sister, Brenda.

"My floater," I offered.

"She is, or shall I say was, married to William Buckley Jr's grandson."

"William Buckley, the columnist?"

"And let us not forget he was the founder of the National Review newspaper."

"Let me guess, based in New York City." The fed looked at me, nodded his head and continued.

"Now allow me to tie all of this up for you. These men are part of the Bilderberg Group."

I searched my memory, but the name was foreign to me. "Doesn't ring a bell," I finally said.

"We'll call it a club, because what it actually is has its own stigma. In a nutshell, it's the world's elite meeting in secret."

I'd like to say Springfield paused to collect his thoughts, but I'm certain he knew exactly what to say. He was trying to lay it out so someone new to the game would understand.

"It is an annual private conference of approximately one hundred fifty of the most influential people from the world of business, finance, academics, media, and even a few presidents and prime ministers. It is believed that the main purpose of this private party of world leaders is to maintain a sort of nobility, mainly in the United States and Europe. Just being rich doesn't get you a seat at this table though; you need to be well placed. You need to have real value."

I thought for a moment. Some people are indeed untouchable. "And the Reagan document," I asked. "What does that do for you?"

"Adds yet another element. Because what the hell is the Convention? With the people involved and what they were able to do, there has to be a tie to the Bilderberg Group. It's another god damn rung in a long ladder."

"So, they're your target."

"No, Mr. Maxim. If secret societies make up the ship and the Bilderberg group the crew, then I'm after its captain. I want the ones pulling their strings. Mr. Maxim, the Convention could very well be the captain of the ship."

"Can we get my friends first?" The fed gave me a short smile and asked the very question I had asked myself.

"What are you going to do after we find them?"

I looked away from my driver, stared out of the windshield, and my first thought was, *I'm getting my friends, and getting off this train*. This had all started with a dame with long legs, and when I thought she was dead, I was happy to be done with all of the nonsense. However, I had been played for a patsy, and that just pissed me off.

*　　*　　*

As the fed drove north on Highway 101, I watched the Pacific Ocean zip by. Occasionally, he regarded his device he had stuck between his legs. 'They stopped,' he finally said.

I didn't ask how far. I just sat patiently and waited. I have said this before, but I really don't like playing second fiddle.

Mark handed me his device and said,

"It looks like we have an option on where to exit and intercept that flashing green square." He pointed to the device. "Pick the best one," He added.

"Exit San Ysidro Road." I said after quickly reviewing it. "It looks like we are going to take it all the way until it ends at the foothills."

"Mr. Maxim, I want to do this gradually. I think it's best to park two full blocks away. Walk up on them slowly."

A few seconds later, he added.

"Me from one direction, you from the other."

Hmmm, that separates us, I thought, but this is the guy who gave my gun back. I nodded my approval and before I knew it, we were exiting San Ysidro Road. It wasn't long before we were approaching the foothills. "Pull over here." I directed Mark to drop me off at San Ysidro Lane. My drop-off spot put me a full two blocks west of the house where the girls were being held. Before I exited the car, I pointed to the device and traced his route with my finger.

I watched Mark turn right and drive down San Ysidro Lane. He turned left and disappeared. This plan put the house between us. I waited several minutes, then walked towards the foothills. I turned right on Las Tunas Road and looked down the street for Mark. After several minutes, I saw his thick frame walking towards me.

Splitting up assured one of us would see anyone trying to leave the residence. However, my partner's movements down the street were very erratic. His switching from one side to the other seemed unnecessary until I noticed an individual sitting in a black Escalade outside of our target house. The driver's arm rested on the window frame; smoke rose from a lit cigarette held loosely between his fingers. From my angle, I could see Mark was a few cars away from someone I knew he was targeting.

Mark was close. I stepped into the street to distract the driver and I walked purposely towards the car waving my arm. Springfield quickly stepped from behind the car, reached in, grabbed the driver, and hit him so hard the car shook. He'd be out for a while. We looked at each other, and if two people were ever on the same page at exactly the same time, it was then. We turned and rushed towards the house.

18

I was a second behind the fed. The big man hit the door, and it seemed to explode. I used my arm to fend off chunks of falling debris. Springfield turned left, and I went right. Without hesitation, he engaged two of the men, and brought them down before they knew what had happened.

The rapid firing of his Glock sent shell casings flying into my periphery while at the same time I pointed my pistol at someone reaching behind their back. A hard kick in my ass told me I had missed someone while coming through the door. The blow shoved me into the person, whom I'm sure, had been reaching for a gun. I brought my left arm up across my chest and jammed my elbow into his throat and pushed him into the wall. A quick glance over my shoulder and I knew, I would be lucky to survive. The attacker, from the rear, already had his gun out, and up. I pushed away from the person I had jammed into the wall, and crouched low in an attempt to get out of the line of fire. As I brought my pistol up, the right side of his headed exploded, Instantly I knew what had happened, Springfield had just saved me. I turned towards the person who was now pulling the gun from behind his back. I repeatedly pressed the trigger on my 1911, sending three, forty-fives in his direction. The nearly half inch chunks of lead easily found their marks, and the force behind them slammed his body into the wall. For a brief moment, as I turned towards Springfield, I watched terror flash across my attackers face while he slid down the wall, smearing the paint with bright red, bloody streaks.

Springfield, who had just given the guy on his left another round to the chest, looked up when suddenly there was a scream. It sent him barreling through another door and into an adjacent room. I swept my colt across the space and checked the men Springfield had just unleashed his fury on. The one on the right was trying to stand, I covered his head with my front sight and pressed the trigger. Springfield hit him, and I was glad to finish him, and a round to his ocular cavity, finished him.

A single gunshot resonated from another part of the house, followed by a scream and then silence.

I hurried into the room to find the fed facing me, his Glock pointing at my head. He quickly lowered it and turned back towards Lorran. She lay motionless, at the foot of the bed. The attacker lay in a growing pool of his own blood, the side of his head gone.

Springfield walked into an adjoining bathroom. I heard the shower curtain being raked across its rail, and seconds later, he stepped back into the bedroom and over to the doc.

'She's okay, just fainted,' he said while scooping her up, and gently laying her on the bed. It was then that I noticed half of her blouse had been torn away. Carefully, Springfield draped the bed sheet over her bare skin. For a long moment, he stared down at Lorran. The concerned look on the feds broad face was very noticeable.

"I'll check the rest of the house." I needed to locate Jessica.

I stepped out into the hallway and took a few steps to the next room. Jessica had been propped in a chair, and her head was slumped to the left side. Blood smeared on the floor and on both armrests didn't give me an easy feeling. The blood that had earlier soaked her shirt seemed to have grown twice in size. I holstered my pistol and quickly stepped towards her and knelt down. I gently cupped her cheek and lightly asked, "Hey, are you ever going to wake up?" When I got no response, I placed my fingers on her neck. The thumping was steady. I picked her up and stepped back into the hallway. "Look who I found," I said while entering the bedroom.

Mark pulled the sheet back and I laid Jessica next to Lorran. With all the sincerity I could muster, I said, "Thanks for the help back there, but more importantly, thanks for finding my friends." He looked at me for several long seconds as if he were making a decision and said,

"DNA."

He read my puzzled look, reached in his pocket, retrieved his device, and handed it to me.

"It's what you had asked about. At the doctor's house, I smeared your friend's blood across the screen. It eventually developed a DNA profile."

I looked down at the device and its blinking screen. Then it hit me. I stated more than asked, "There can't possibly be a satellite that can track someone's DNA?"

He glanced over at the girls and then back at me. While leaning towards the window, he offered,

"You'd be shocked at what satellites can do."

His answer only left me with questions, but it answered one for sure: Mark Springfield was a bona fide spook. As I was thinking about his *not working for the DIA* comment, I watched him pull a pillowcase off a pillow and drape it over the head of the dead guy.

"What now?" He asked. "How do you want to play this?"

While pondering the question, I looked back at the door we had come through. It had been split in two, with one half of it hanging from hinges that had been partially torn away from the jamb. I glanced up at the fed, whom returned a slight smirk. Mark Springfield cannot only handle a pistol, he is his own god damn battering ram.

I removed my 1911, pulled an extra magazine from a pouch on the side of my holster, and swapped it for the one in my gun. Honestly, I didn't know. If I could take the girls and leave without a worry, I would. I looked at Springfield and before I could answer, a faint call came from the bed.

"Shawn!"

It was Jessica and she sounded confused. I quickly replied, "Jess, I'm here." I stepped over to her and knelt next to the bed. "Hey, how are you?"

'Shawn?' She asked. Shawn! Why would she ask for Shawn? "Jessica, Shawn's not here." Her eyes fluttered open while she lifted her head. The first thing they focused on was the hulking man standing behind me. Startled, she asked,

"Who are you...Wait, I know you. Dick, we know him!"

"At least you know me," I chuckled. "It's okay. He helped me find the two of you." I nodded towards Lorran. Jessica rolled her head in the doc's direction; however, she couldn't keep her eyes open. Before she drifted off, I asked. "Why do you think Shawn is here?" After a few long seconds, she answered.

"Shawn? I called him from your friend's house."

Okay, now I was confused. Jessica had Shawn's number and even thought to call him from Lorran's house. So, I asked, "Jessica, my Shawn? Detective Vanderwerff, Shawn Vanderwerff."

With a thin smile, she answered,

"He's not just your Shawn."

I stood. While staring down at Jessica, I tried to pull it all together. I turned towards the fed and explained. "LA Detective Shawn Vanderwerff. He's a friend of mine." Suddenly a thought occurred to me. I fished my phone from my pocket and checked it. Nothing, nothing from Shawn. Yeah, that was odd. I sensed Springfield was waiting, and I thought he was waiting on me. Finally, he said.

"And then they were kidnapped."

Springfield gave me a hard look and all I could say was, "I know, I know!" It was taking me a minute, but I was getting there. I had one more question for Jessica before I let her sleep. "Did you tell Shawn your location?" She gave a quiet, reassuring, 'no,' and drifted off. Inwardly I felt relieved until Lorran spoke up and uttered,

"I did."

Wait, what?! I looked over at Lorran who was pushing herself up on her elbows while looking around the room. She sat up completely and rubbed both hands over her face. The big man reached over my shoulder, handed Lorran a wet rag, and offered a warm smile. She repeated the wiping action and continued with.

"Your friend handed me her phone and I gave the detective my address, he said he was a friend of yours."

"And then they were kidnapped," The fed repeated.

"God damn it, not Shawn!" I snapped. I stopped myself, held out my hand as though I was patting the air and quietly repeated. "Not Shawn."

"Give me Vanderwerff's cell phone number."

As soon as Springfield asked for Shawn's number, it cemented him as a suspect. However, and I don't mind saying it, I still can't wrap my head around it. I know people, I read them every day. And since our first meeting when I stepped into his crime scene, I took him for a straight shooter, a methodical and solid detective. *Not someone that could ever be involved in any type of nefarious activity*, I thought to myself while looking around the room... Anybody else, but not Shawn.

* * *

Well, that answered *the what am I going to do next* question. I was going to clear Shawn of all of this...or hold him accountable. I holstered my gun, looked over at the fed, and asked, "Thoughts?"

He quickly answered with,

"Call your friend and ask him one question... Why?"

"Did I do something wrong," Lorran suddenly asked.

"No, you didn't know." Springfield soothingly answered as if already condemning Shawn.

I looked over at Mark with a raised eyebrow. He was nicer to Lorran than needed. I looked back at Lorran who was giving the big man a smile. Apparently, there was some sort of attraction. I brushed off the thought, slid my phone out of my pocket, and pressed Shawn's number. He picked up on the second ring, but never answered. I turned, faced Springfield, and spoke evenly into the phone. "Why?" The silence on his end sent a thunderous message, and I was ready to disconnect when he said,

"Can we meet? And when I say 'we,' I mean just you and me."

Springfield was right... God damn it. "Looks like we should. Pick a spot." Springfield sliced his fingers across his throat. I knew exactly what he meant and ended the call. "That wasn't even twenty seconds," I said.

"Call him back."

As I was about to call, my phone rang. When I answered, Shawn only spoke two words and then hung up. It was a place we had visited many times. I looked up at Springfield and said,

"Traveler's Tavern. It's not far from here. It's just off the 154, the San Marcos Pass." Shawn and I had made many trips to the old Tavern after a day on the lake.

Well so much for getting off the train, and the funny thing was, the only person I could trust was the fed.

"How long to get there?" He asked

"Twenty minutes. And the girls," I added. The fed paused, almost like he wasn't sure of the next move. "You stay here with Lorran and Jessica." I said. "I'll meet Shawn." I hesitated to let the plan sink in.

We stared at each other for a long moment, and then he finally said, "I'll take good care of them, and our friend in the car."

"I trust you will."

19

My first thought as I raced onto the 101 was that Shawn picked the tavern because he was close. It was no longer a question on whether or not he was involved. He was not only involved, he was responsible for the girls being kidnapped.

And why didn't I know about him and Jessica? Two years ago, I had had a small Christmas party, just a group of close friends. It hadn't seemed the two of them even spoke. However, aside from that why keep the relationship from me, why?

It didn't take long before I was peeling off onto the 154. With light traffic on the one lane mountainous road, I would be there in fifteen minutes.

I crossed over the Cold Spring Canyon arched bridge and a few minutes later I made a right onto Paradise road and dropped down into the canyon. Travelers Tavern was an old rest stop complete with its own jail. It dated back to the late eighteen hundreds and now operated as a quaint restaurant and bar. It had the charm of, well, an old tavern.

I drove by the tavern while looking for Shawn's car or anyone out of place. Not seeing anything, I flipped around and parked on the tavern's side of the road so I could make a quick getaway when the time came. If experience as taught me anything, it was that driving straight got me out of binds more quickly and safely than making high speed skidding U-turns.

I slowly walked towards the structure while scanning the tree line. Suddenly, Shawn stepped from behind the old jail. Instinct drove my hand towards my pistol. However, his hands were empty, so I left my Colt holstered. In that instant a slight chill went up my spine. I realized he had had the drop on me. Yeah, that felt strange.

Shawn tilted his head towards one of the outdoor benches and said 'Join me.' A quick glance and I noticed two glass mugs full of beer sitting on one of the tables at the edge of the outside dining area.

"Just like old times," I stated.

"No, Dick, nothing will ever be the same."

Shawn walked away from the jail and around the table, taking a seat at the end with his back against the road. I stepped towards the table, keeping him in view. We sat across from each other; I faced the dirt road. We stared at each other. I spoke first. "Mind telling me what the hell is going on? And when we get through that, mind telling me why your relationship with Jessica was a secret?" He tilted his beer, studied the bottom of the glass, then took a long drink and offered.

"You're not gonna like it."

"God damn it, I already don't like it!"

"The answers to your questions are the same. You know the old saying, keep your friends close and your enemies closer?"

I shook my head, "What are you talking about? Since when are we enemies?" I watched Shawn take another drink, the expression on his face turned... cold. His next comment took me by surprise.

"You have a document we want."

He had cut right to the chase and had to be talking about what I had been calling the Reagan document. Finally, I took a mouthful of beer, not because I was in the mood to drink, but it was to cover up my surprised look. How could he possibly be involved in this? He waited for me to set my beer down and continued.

"Someone gained access to a safe deposit box they were never meant to have. And that someone was using the information as blackmail."

I felt like I had been clubbed on the top of my head. He knew about the safe deposit box.

"And your client wanted in on the action. She wasn't quite sure what the action was, but she noticed a big uptick in her husband's lifestyle. We were able to scare off the first three PIs she hired. And Jessica was just being herself and offended the woman. However, when she hired you, I knew there was going to be a problem."

And then it hit me. What Springfield had said about them knowing me... Shawn was that connection.

"Shawn, how are you involved in this?" I blurted.

"This is the part you're not going to like. I've been using you and Jessica as kind of informants. The information from some of the cases you've worked have really helped our organization over the years."

"I can't possibly be hearing this right. I feel like I'm in an alternate universe. Are you telling me our friendship has been a sham? Our fishing trips were for intelligence gathering?"

"Mostly, but I do like to fish," He said with a smirk.

I paused and felt the anger grow. "Why bring Jessica into all of this?"

"Another PI means more information."

"But why keep it a secret?"

"I told her to keep our relationship from you because I was afraid, sooner or later, you would catch on. And here we are, Dick. I wondered how this moment would play out."

Then I asked a question I really wanted an answered to. "And where does Springfield fit into all of this?"

Shawn took another drink of beer and answered. "Yes, Mark Springfield, a royal pain in my ass. He seemed to come out of nowhere." After a long pause, he added. "He'll be dealt with."

I shook off the tunnel vision I was developing while staring at the stranger sitting across from me. I looked around the outdoor space and made a mental note of a man and woman sitting at a far table and a family who had walked across the dirt parking lot and stepped inside of the restaurant. Two employees were carrying a large tray of sizzling barbecued tri-tip from the side of the building. There were more cars than there were people.

I looked back at Shawn, and I had to know, so I asked, "Tell me you didn't try to have Jessica killed."

He answered with a statement. "You asked me if I knew of the LAPDs Public Disorder Intelligence Division."

"Yeah, I remember you told me you didn't know much about it. Another lie, I'll assume. Like a fool I asked you. You knew right from the start I was onto something." He wasn't going to answer my question.

"My uncle was part of it, and yes, in name it was disbanded. It lives on, Dick, stronger than ever, still operating under the founder's original intent. However, unfortunately, he collected so much information it had gotten him killed."

There was no remorse in Shawn's voice, so I reminded him of some of the details. "Let's not forget the fact that Russia shot down flight double-o-seven with two hundred and sixty-eight innocent folks on board to get one person." But he just shook his head and with a shrug callously said,

"Details."

I felt my face twist with unfathomable disgust, and clearly Shawn read it, he continued with,

"Don't be so hard on yourself, my friend. You were behind right from the start."

"Jesus Christ, Shawn, when did you become so heartless?" He didn't answer, but gave me another shrug. I continued with, "Tell me... all of this...is it worth it?" I didn't give him time to answer. I just spat, "What the hell happened to you?" I started to lose control, and his answer drove me closer to the edge.

"If you gaze long enough into the abyss, the abyss will gaze back into you."

"Nietzsche!" I almost shouted. "You're F-ing quoting Friedrich Nietzsche?" The smirk on Shawn's face made my blood boil. He had gotten under my skin, and he knew it.

"That German was a smart man," he added.

"But he lost his mind at forty-five," I reminded him. Shawn just stared and gave me a toothy grin. With the ruse of shifting uncomfortably in my seat, I gave the area another once over while releasing the mug's handle and wrapping my hand around the glass. I took several deep breaths and tried to settle my inner torment and focus, then I asked, "Of all places, why bring me here? Why tell me all of this?"

"We needed to make sure you weren't followed. Dick, I wanted you alone."

"But we aren't alone, are we?" I said with a slight nod towards the couple sitting across the lot.

Shawn took the last swig of his beer, set the mug down harder than he needed to, and wiped over his mouth with the back of his hand, and said,

"We want the file, but either way, Dick, you're not leaving this canyon alive."

20

n the blink of an eye the betrayal I felt turned to rage. I acted fast and already had the first move planned. I pushed up from the table with my left hand, stepped over the bench seat, and launched the glass mug at Shawn's head. In that same motion, I pulled my 1911 and swept it across the lot towards the couple standing up from the table, both reaching inside their jackets. Everyone at the tavern was the enemy; I trusted no one...even if they were holding a baby.

In that instant, it was Vietnam all over again. I was trapped, or call it an ambush; either way I was the target of an assassination. Hatchet flew us into a small village to retrieve intel. I had had an uneasy feeling from the start. Five minutes after the skids hit the foliage, three of us walked into a small village. A young woman, holding a baby, walked across a dirt road and straight towards us. The look on her face emitted a determination that instantly turned to fear. She hid the grenade between her chest and the child. Suddenly, there was small-arms fire. It was the only thing that had saved me. A bullet tore through my neck, flipping me over a small embankment.

As I hit the ground, the hand grenade detonated, and the blast killed everyone within twenty feet, everyone. This is the part where I said I have seen things no man should ever see. I physically recovered from being shot. However, it took some time to mentally recover from the nightmares that always showed, in vivid color, pieces of human flesh lying on and all around me. The carnage of war stays with you the rest of your life.

Other than Hatchet, who had waited in the running helo, there were three of us. I was helped back to the Huey by the only surviving teammate. However, Jackson, a scrawny eighteen-year-old from the Bronx, took the brunt of the explosion. He had tried to stop the woman's advancements and was almost on top of her four seconds after she released the spoon, arming and setting the delay for the grenade. Two Hueys, a few minutes behind us, with their blazing M60 machine guns laid down suppressive fire, giving us the valuable minutes, we needed to escape.

Reflexively, I presented and returned fire with the same gun as I now hold in my hand. I fired at anything that moved. Call it shock, call it feeling your heart pumping blood out of your body and you just wanting to live. The things you have done in the past come rushing back and play out in front of you. It was surreal; I had a war going on around me and all I could see was my childhood. I knew I was going to die. However, by some miracle I survived. And here I was again, set up. It felt so much like Vietnam, the scar on my neck burned.

I knew Shawn's slammed beer mug was a call to action. I had been at this game long enough to know the signs. I no longer smelled the barbecue; I smelled the jungle.

My 1911 barked three times before I swung it back across the street, aligning the sights on a man I noticed out of the corner of my eye. He was stepping from the tree line and raising a pistol, but he went down after a single shot. I kept Shawn in my periphery while I reengaged the first two who seemed to be scrambling to get away from the open table. I pressed the trigger until the slide locked back.

I quickly swapped magazines and sent another two chunks of lead down range, but it was for naught as my attackers both lay over the table, their blood running off the bench and soaking the ground below. I lowered my pistol and pointed it at Shawn's chest. But I couldn't do it. I couldn't press the trigger. I justified it because the glass mug had found its mark and laid Shawn out cold. I turned and pointed my pistol down the road. Two women walking towards the tavern screeched, turned, and ran screaming the other way. Two shots rang out from behind the old jail. One hit its mark, but I wasn't the target, it was Shawn.

He took a round in the gut, and the way he was bleeding I knew he would never wake up from being hit with the mug. But why him, why shoot one of their own? Then a slug slammed into my shoulder and drove me to the ground. I crawled under the bench and with my good shoulder pushed the table up on its side. Three more rounds pelted the wood, the third hit an edge and sent splinters across my back. I couldn't lift my right arm.

With my left hand I grabbed my pistol and peered out from the left bottom side of the table. I expected to see someone rushing my position. However, it was quiet, too quiet. In battle you need to act decisively, so I rolled to my right, staying inside the protection of the table, then I shoved my pistol into the dirt to help push me off the ground and sprinted across the lot while returning fire in the direction of the jail, more so to assure my pistol wouldn't jam from being stuck in the grime.

I jumped on and slid across the wooden top, using my feet to push the two off the table and onto the ground. I landed hard and almost lost my grip on the 1911. I couldn't feel my shoulder, but I knew the pain would find me. I twisted in the dirt and clutched the top of the woman's shirt. I dragged her lifeless body and stacked it on top of her partner to act as a shield. Then I patted down both of their pockets hoping to find anything useful. However, lying under the table was a phone. I belly crawled around my barrier and retrieved it, and as I did,

I noticed movement from Shawn's direction. I couldn't believe what I was seeing. He was trying to push himself off the ground. Then, the jungle of Vietnam returned.

It started with a high-pitched whine, and then thumping. The rotors of the helicopter beat the air half a football field behind the tavern. I pulled myself all the way under the table and waited, waited for my wooden shield to be bombarded with lead. I looked up through the cracks in the slats and watched the helo fly up to and hover over the tavern. I saw, more than heard, the muzzle blasts. A shooter from the helicopter targeted the gunman hiding on the side of the jail. I watched the muzzle light up multiple times. I waited for my turn in the barrel, but it never came. The helo kicked itself around and the next shot was in Shawn's direction. Instinctively, I wanted to race over and drag him to safety, but it wasn't to be.

The change in the rotors' whine told me the Helo was headed out. I glanced over at my old friend. He laid motionless, spread out in the dirt. I knew this time he wasn't getting up. The ache I felt in my gut was unexpected.

I felt so damn confused. Honestly, I didn't know what or how to think. Shawn had threatened my life, but now...he was gone. I took careful aim at the helo and let loose a volley of rounds. But only in Hollywood does that ever work. It had tilted its nose and headed east. It was gone as quickly as it had appeared.

21

Now I had a problem. I had five dead people, one of them a cop, and to make matters worse, a detective. I knew this had only taken minutes to play out, I also knew that the police were about fifteen minutes away.

I walked over to Shawn, knelt down, and laid my hand on his shoulder. The pale color of his skin and blank stare through opened eyes told me I would never get an answer. My friend would never be able to tell me what the hell was truly going on. Yeah, after all of this, I called him my friend. It's hard to erase years of friendship. I have a hard time understanding it all. How could I have been so fooled? But I would deal with that later. Now, now it was time to go. I stood, but before I turned away, I noticed an outline on Shawn's back pocket...a tell-tale sign of a cell phone. I knelt back down and worked it out of his trousers. I stood slowly and worked my knee back and forth. I spent too much time on the damn ground and my joints had started to stiffen. Yeah, getting older sucks. I gave the tavern's lot another quick look, turned, and with a slight limp walked to my car.

I never saw the two women who had run screaming back down the road, but once I was back in my car, I constantly looked around.

Slowly, I drove up the winding road, forcing myself not to look at Shawn as I passed the park. I eventually reached Highway 154, turned left, and headed back down the mountain towards Santa Barbara. It wasn't until I was accelerating onto the 101 south on-ramp, fifteen minutes later, that I saw three highway patrol cruisers racing towards the 154. They were for me, but I would be well outside of Santa Barbara before they arrived at the Tavern.

I was sure Springfield would remove the women from the house. Not just to get away from the carnage, but because Santa Barbara was a town that would not let gunshots go unreported. I picked up my phone and hesitated. I realized I didn't have Springfield's number, but I had the girls. I called Lorran, since she had seemed more awake when I left. The fed answered on the first ring and ended the call after he said,

"Mrs. Makenzie's house."

The doc's house! I thought. They had been kidnapped from there. Why would we return there? It only took me a moment to figure it out. The document. The fed asked me to stash it at the house and now he wanted it.

I rounded the last corner of one of the sleepy bedroom communities that lay on the outskirts of Santa Barbara, and found myself pressing the accelerator pedal harder than I needed to. I backed off so I didn't draw any undue attention. It had taken twenty minutes since I left the tavern, but I finally had the Pacific Ocean fill my windshield. The vastness and rhythm of the sea usually makes me forget my problems. Not today, today I found myself with my head on a swivel, sweeping the highway looking for the stereotypical black, SUV that may have me in their sights. Occasionally, I strained my neck, pushing my head up against the windshield to search the horizon for any menacing helicopters.

Halfway to Ventura, I finally relaxed. I felt myself sitting deeper into the seat. Occasionally, I lifted my shoulder, wondering why the pain had subsided. I still remained vigilant and used my mirrors to scan the roadway and sky, but at least now I didn't look like a cartoon character while I did it.

This was new territory for me, and I knew for sure most of what had happened at the tavern was filmed, cell phones were everywhere. Hopefully, it was sporadic. I could also bank on witnesses to be unreliable with descriptions. Fingers crossed.

Although five people were killed, I could only put three of those notches on my gun. Well, that is if there was room for three more, hypothetically speaking, of course. The search would intensify once it was discovered that a police detective was dead. The cops don't take it lightly when they lose one of their own.

Suddenly, the buzz of a cell phone caused me to look where I had tossed the two phones, the front passenger's seat. The buzzing phone belonged to Shawn. I flipped it over, expecting to see a name, but only a phone number was displayed and underneath it the word, 'Status!' I looked at the number again and felt the sequence was familiar. It was, in fact, too familiar.

As I drove south, it started to gnaw at me, but without the full use of my right arm, I couldn't safely manipulate the phone, so I exited Bates Road, turned right onto Rincon Point, and made another quick right onto South Via Real. I continued up the road to a small park that overlooked the Pacific. There were only a few visitors, so finding an empty spot to pull into would be easy. I turned left into a parking space, shifted into park, and stared at the ocean as I searched for an answer from within the waves. The more I thought about the number, the more familiar it seemed. I removed my phone and punched in the number. As I expected, a name appeared on the screen.

I scanned the ocean once again, waiting for an answer. And then the ocean spoke. I grabbed Shawn's phone, selected the text and typed, *one wounded, one dead including Maxim. No document, but know where it is. Going for it now.* The one-word question needed a short reply. Moments after I hit send, the tell-tale signs of a return text being written displayed on the screen. Seconds after it appeared, it stopped as though the sender decided not to reply, which was okay with me.

I waved my goodbyes to the ocean, backed out of the parking spot, and headed back to the 101.

I'd like to say I was shocked at the name that appeared on my phone, but I wasn't. All I could say was, "Gotcha!"

22

Picking up Shawn's phone had been enlightening. With the exception of my shoulder that now hurt like hell, it made the rest of the trip to Doc Makenzie's house seem to go by in a blur. I pulled in the driveway, stepped out of the car, and walked directly into the house. Springfield was standing to the left of the window that overlooked the front yard. As I stepped through the entrance, he pointed to a door that was ajar. I stepped over to it and knocked, then pushed it open and stepped into a room that had bookcases covering two adjacent walls, making it look more like a library than a small office.

Both women stood when I entered the room. I went straight to Lorran, hating what I had to tell Jessica. I wrapped my arms around the doc and said, "I'm so sorry to bring you into this."

I heard her laugh quietly and offer, "My dad always said you were good at finding trouble." She pushed back slightly and with a sly grin added, "Mark's been keeping us safe."

"Aren't we friendly," I said. However, the humor I found in it was short-lived. I turned towards Jessica and felt a growing lump in my throat. I walked over, reached out, and grabbed both of her hands. I held them lightly and said, "Shawn's...

"Don't say it, Dick. Don't say it."

"Ms. Sleeman, Jessica. You need to hear it."

The comment came from Springfield whose frame now filled the doorway. Looking back at her tormented face, I continued. "I'm sorry, Jessica, but Shawn is dead." She straightened up, closed her eyes, and took a deep breath. Several long seconds had passed when she opened her tear-soaked eyes and questioningly asked.

"Tell me you didn't kill him."

"I did not." I was relieved to say it. I gave her a hug and then helped her back to the chair. I turned to Lorran who was noticing my blood-soaked shoulder. "It's just a scratch." I offered matter-of-factly.

"No, Dick. I have been watching. You can hardly move it."

"I'll be fine. Can we get Jessica some water, perhaps a sedative?" I watched Lorran disappear into her makeshift office, then I knelt down beside Jessica. She had her head buried in her hands and she was lightly sobbing.

"Shawn was using the two of us." I quietly offered as some sort of justification. Jessica lifted her head out of her hands and said,

"Shortly after we started dating, he asked if you and I ever discussed work, asked if we compared notes. He also asked if I'd keep our relationship between the two of us."

"That didn't seem off to you?"

"I guess at the time I never really thought about it."

"You never thought to tell me, Jess?"

"Honestly, Dick, it was fun knowing something you didn't."

"I have a confession to make."

The statement from the fed took us by surprise. We both looked up at him questioningly, he sounded...guilty.

"I was the one who visited your dad."

"And left me the envelope?" Jessica snapped.

"Yes. I wanted you to think twice about pursuing this case."

"You scared the shit out of me!"

"I did it hoping to protect you. I'm sorry."

"But how did you..."

'Here, Jessica, take these.' Lorran offered while handing her two pills and a glass of water. I stood and let the doc do her thing. I was grateful for her timing. As I backed away, I gave Springfield an even gaze. Before I could say anything, Lorran grabbed my good forearm and said,

"You're coming with me. I want to take a look at that shoulder."

I gave her a warm smile and, more forcibly than I should have, said, "Not yet. I need to speak to Mr. Springfield, or are we on a first name basis?" I added returning her sly look.

* * *

I turned towards Mark and pointed to the living room and closed the door when we stepped out of the office. While handing him a phone, I said, "I took this off of Detective Vanderwerff. When I was driving back here, that number and text pinged on the screen." Springfield glanced at the screen and said,

"And?"

I took the phone, handed him mine, and said, "The number seemed very familiar so I punched it into my phone. This is what came up." I watched a thin grin start on the fed's face when he said,

"Elizabeth Tully."

I shook my head and added. "Detective Vanderwerff told me Mrs. Tully wanted access to the safe deposit box because her husband was living the high life. He lied. She wanted the document, but her husband was the one who got to the safe deposit box by mistake. Obviously, she and Shawn were working together."

"I don't think it was a mistake, Dick. I believe Luciano Tully figured it out."

I thought for a moment and then it hit me. Elizabeth Tully married a banker to keep her family firmly entrenched in the financial world. Mark had also told me her father was the retired president of one of the Federal Reserve Banks and in, of all places, New York, one of the world's financial hubs. I looked at Mark and stated, "But Tully's not just any banker." *No, he can't be,* I thought. "He became very dangerous when he found that document. I know... some of his people tried to kill me."

I walked across the room trying to put the rest of it together. "He surrounded himself with a security detachment so he had to know what it really meant."

"Mr. Maxim, are you aware that there are twelve Federal Reserve Banks? And overseeing those banks is a mix of seven men and women called the board of governors."

"Doing what?" I asked.

"Overseeing the entire United States banking system." Mark answered, then continued with, "You might be right. Tully's more than just a bank president. He stumbled across the document that was meant for his wife and knew exactly what he had. He's tied..."

A thought hit me, and before Mark could finish his comment, I offered, "What if both Elizabeth and her husband are part of the well-connected and neither one knows about the other. But why wouldn't they know about each other?"

"Because like any good organization that is keeping a secret, they compartmentalized their people." Mark answered with authority.

Yes, Springfield was absolutely correct. Not everyone could see the big picture.

"Let's say Elizabeth Tully's family is somehow associated with the board of governors." Mark continued shaking his finger in the air to no one. "And let's say some members of the board, both past and present, are part of a group known as the Convention."

"Which is exactly what the Reagan document calls out," I added. "The funny thing is Elizabeth McDonough married Luciano Tully to keep her family in the banking and financial world. Little did she know, her husband may be part of the same organization. Both of them unaware of the other's connection," I concluded.

"And both not wanting to kill the other," Mark added.

"Sounds like true love to me," I quipped. "It was purely coincidental that she had picked him."

"Her sister Brenda Buckley must really have become a liability, perhaps a rift in the family, so they killed two birds with one stone. They murdered her and got you to act."

"And it worked," I sighed. After a long pause Marked added.

"The convention could very well be that captain of the ship."

When I first met Elizabeth Tully, I wondered if marrying into money had changed her, but she did not marry into it, she had been born into it. Whatever happened to her happened because her parents wanted it to happen.

Now it was Mark's turn to show concern. He nodded towards my shoulder and asked.

"Should Lorran look at that?"

I shook my head, but with a slight tilt, grunted, "Perhaps." Now it burned more than hurt. "But first things first," I said. I paid another visit to Lorran's couch and retrieved the envelope, then walked out and handed it to Mark who coolly tossed it on a small table. Then I walked back into Lorran's office, over to a small credenza, and pulled open the lower left-hand door and removed a bottle of Bourbon. On the adjacent shelves were four crystal tumblers turned upside down and four stemless wine glasses. I removed two of the tumblers, turned, and walked back out to the living room. I handed the glasses to Mark and filled them from a bottle I had gifted to Lorran months ago. I took one from the fed, clinked it against his, and said, "Thanks again for finding my friends."

I enjoy a good Bourbon, and as I downed it, I thought of Shawn and our first meeting. The woman, lying dead in his crime scene, was someone who had recently hired me to investigate her brother.

Unfortunately, she had been shot three times, and thrown through a window five stories up. I learned later that those crimes did not sit very well with the detective. However, he was methodical in his approach, and three days later, with the help of yours truly, solved the crime. We forged a friendship that had lasted until the tavern. The thought of it made me sick to my stomach.

I refilled my glass and in two gulps it was gone. I raised my empty tumbler to Mark, then set it down on a table next to the manila envelope and said, "Don't go anywhere," turned, and walked into the doc's home treatment room.

Lorran was already laying out the tools of her trade. She took perverse pleasure in making a point, so I knew the hypodermic with its longer than required needle was to teach me a lesson.

"It sounded like you were getting into my liquor cabinet?"

"Is that size needle really required?" I asked changing the subject. Indiana Jones hates snakes, and of all things, I hate needles. After giving me a sideways look, she reached up, helped me out of my shoulder holster and then draped the rig over a loveseat. The doc sat me down, picked up a pair of scissors, and proceeded to cut a slit up the sleeve of my shirt. Continuing around the shoulder across the back and down the sides. Then gently she removed my entire shirt. After a short exam, she said,

"Jesus, Richard! Don't tell me that doesn't hurt like hell."

"I'm sure it will when you jam that needle in my arm," I protested. "Be nice, Makenzie!" Yeah, I called her by her last name, because I knew what she was about to do would send a jolt down my spine. Did I learn a lesson? You bet I did. The next time I'd check myself into a hospital.

23

I don't know if it was the sound of the music that caused my eyes to flutter open or the throbbing I felt in my arm. It took several long seconds to make sense of it all, and as I did, a large round light fixture came into focus. I tried to move, but quickly discovered my arm had been strapped across my chest. I was reclined in the dentist chair, which I didn't remember being moved to. I twisted myself up and swung my feet over the side of the chair. I sat there for a minute collecting myself, slowly remembering how and why I had ended up there in the first place. The music I heard was pleasant; the volume was just enough to be more soothing than annoying.

I tried to stand, but quickly sat back down. From the doorway behind me, in a low calming voice, the doc uttered,

"You may want to give yourself another five, ten minutes."

I rubbed my left hand over my face and through my hair. I watched the doc walk across the room to the sink and fill a glass with water. She turned and while walking towards me offered a caring smile. Then she handed me the glass.

"I didn't know I was going to be put out," I protested.

"There was too much damage, Dick. I knew you would object about being put under, so I didn't ask."

"This was not the time to put me under," I firmly stated.

"Mark protected us." She said with a grin.

Suddenly a memory, a vision if you will, cued by Lorran's mention of Springfield pushed its way up through my foggy mind. I must have regained consciousness for a short period while in the chair. I remembered seeing Lorran and the fed in a long embrace.

I pushed the memory down and asked, "My arm, how bad was it?"

"The top of your arm, inches in front of where it meets the shoulder was shredded. You were lucky. Quarter inch lower and you'd need a shoulder replacement. I find it hard to believe you waited so long to have me look at it."

I gave the doc a crooked smile and quipped, "Well, the bourbon helped."

I looked around the room, located my gun, and then asked, "Where is Springfield?"

"Mark?"

Hmmm… The way she said Mark, along with my vision, was telling, so I asked, "There seemed to be some sort of macabre connection between you two. I noticed it at the house and if I'm not mistaken, you two were hugging earlier, what gives?"

"Well, I don't know about macabre. However, there is something. I felt it the first time I looked at him. As far as the hug…"

Lorran stop, smiled, and added,

"I was thanking him for saving us."

"Wouldn't a simple thank you suffice?"

"No, Dick, not after everything that has happened. And don't worry about my love life."

I gave the doc my best fatherly look and asked, "and where is your Casanova?"

"He's gone, took the envelope with him."

"Honestly, I'm glad I don't have it."

"He promised to take good care of it. Oh, there's something else."

I watched Lorran pull a folded piece of paper from her back pocket. She handed it to me and said,

"Mark wanted me to give this to you when you woke up."

I took the paper, unfolded it, and chuckled after reading the first few words.

'You're welcome for the help.' The letter continued with.

'Dick, the Reagan document sheds light onto something that I have been working on for a while. However, there's no reason for you to continue.

There will be no reason to pursue you if you don't have the letter. The further you and Jessica are away from this, the safer you both will be.

The scene was cleaned up at the tavern by the same folks who had cleaned Jessica's house. Treat the girls to a nice dinner and put this all behind you. I'll take it from here.'

My arms dropped onto my lap after I read the last line, which said: 'P.S. I sent the helicopter.'

Shit, that was why he hesitated back at the house. He wasn't trying to formulate a plan; he was wondering if he could get me help in time. I gave Lorran a grin and asked. "Are you going to see our fed again?" She turned beet red and said,

"Well, I got more than a hug, he jotted down his phone number, too."

How do you find a boyfriend in the midst of all of this? I thought. Lorran never seemed to be one who acted impulsively. I thought of her dad, John. He was a hard-hitting, full throttle warrior. He flew his Huey as though he was invincible. However, he was the only pilot we ever wanted to fly with. He was our guy, but truth be told we were young and all of us thought we wore Superman's cape.

I looked at Lorran in a different light. She was a woman through and through, and she seemed to have the same toughness as her dad. In fact, so tough it appeared she may have broken through what I could only assume was Springfield's very hard shell.

Jesus, Hatchet would be proud of her.

* * *

The shooting range.
Two weeks later

Fifteen minutes of dry practice and one hundred and fifty live rounds later, I finally felt comfortable with my target. My shoulder and the huge bruise on the right side of my buttocks, compliments from sliding across the table and the hard landing that ensued, finally felt as good as one could expect after two weeks. What did I learn from my latest case? That I needed more practice shooting with my non-dominate hand.

I have not heard a word from Mr. Springfield. And Jessica has not been taking my calls. I'll give her more of the only thing that will truly help, time.

Is this case finished you ask? In a word, yes, it's over. However, I'm far from done. Over the last couple of weeks, I have had time to reflect on the past events. I know the players and what they are capable of. I'll let you in on a little secret, I'm going after them.

I'm a PI for Christ's sake, might as well act like one.

THE END

FOR NOW

Be polite, and respectful, but have a plan to kill everyone you meet. - Mark Springfield

9 781733 977258